WICKED HARVEST

A DEWBERRY FARM MYSTERY

KAREN MACINERNEY

GRAY WHALE PRESS

Books in the Dewberry Farm Mystery Series

Killer Jam

Fatal Frost

Deadly Brew

Mistletoe Murder

Dyeing Season

Wicked Harvest

❀ Created with Vellum

_As_ I stared at what was left of my beautiful, once-verdant rows of crookneck squash, pumpkins, buttercup squash, and cucumbers, I reflected on the vicissitudes of farming. Where healthy plants had sprawled the week before, now the ground was covered with skeletal leaves and worm-riddled fruit. I nudged a pumpkin with my foot, and the soft flesh gave beneath my boot.

It had been the third hottest summer on record in Buttercup, and most of the local farmers and ranchers had spent most of it praying for rain. Apparently, it had worked.

Too well.

After the blistering heat of the summer, the warm deluge that arrived in September had lasted for more than a week, providing a perfect breeding ground for the dreaded melon worm, a recent invader from South Texas. Last week, there had been rows of gleaming vegetables and lush, healthy vines. Now, I had rows and rows of wormy, dead plants to deal with... and not a whole lot to take to market.

I sighed and glanced over toward where Blossom and her daughter were grazing. Thanks to the summer drought,

I'd had to pay for more hay than I'd anticipated, which had wiped out most of the profit from the dairy part of the farm business. Soon, all the goats and cows would be pregnant again, and the milk supply would dry up while the moms devoted their resources to their growing offspring. Good for the farm in the long run, but not so good for the short-term finances.

As I dug up a squash plant and tried not to dwell on gloomy thoughts, the sound of hammering floated across the pasture to me. I glanced over toward the Ulrich house, the hundred-and-fifty-year-old wooden house I had been talked into moving onto the property several months ago. It had belonged to one of Buttercup's first families, and I'd been talked into saving the historic structure. Thanks to a few small windfalls along with my improving business sense, renovations were moving along—slowly, but moving—and I was hoping to have the place ready to rent out in time for the spring antique fair down the road in Round Top. Ed Mandel, a local carpenter, had braced the house and was replacing the rotting studs; I'd already picked out tile for the bathroom and paint colors for the upstairs walls, and I was looking forward to refinishing the old oak floors. Today, Ed's young assistant Nick Schmidt was replacing some of the decaying wood; from what I could tell, things were going smoothly, and Ed had assured me we were on schedule for a spring opening.

At least that was one thing that was going right, I thought as I shoveled another wormy pumpkin into the growing pile.

I'd taken care of the pumpkins and was halfway down the first row of squash—I was planning to remove and destroy the plants so that there was less chance of larvae staying hidden in the soil—when there was a creaking sound from the little house. As I looked back at it, the building seemed to slew to the left, toward the creek; a moment later, Nick shot out of the front door.

I gripped the shovel and held my breath, hoping the whole thing wouldn't collapse. It seemed to move a bit more, then stopped. I threw down the shovel and hurried over to where Nick was standing, hands on his head, his face the color of milk.

"What happened?" I asked.

"I must have done something wrong," he said. "I was taking out a rotting board, and then the whole thing kind of... well..."

"Almost fell over," I supplied. "But it didn't," I added, trying for an optimistic tone, "and you're safe and sound."

"Right," he said in a weak voice, and I found myself wondering if my insurance policy covered buildings collapsing during renovation.

"Maybe we should call Ed," I suggested.

"Yes. We should," he agreed, but made no move for his phone. I pulled mine out of my back pocket and dialed, but got voice mail.

"Hey, Ed," I said. "It looks like the house is kind of... well, tipping over," I said. "In fact, it almost collapsed on Nick," I said, glancing at the young man, "and I'm worried that if we have wind, the whole thing might go over. So if you give me a call and come check it out as soon as possible, that would be great," I added, and left my number for good measure before hanging up.

"I don't understand what happened," Nick said, a groove between his bushy eyebrows. Although he was only eighteen, he seemed older, somehow; maybe because the hard work had gotten rid of any teenaged gangliness. "We braced the whole thing."

Together, we walked around the house, inspecting the cables Ed and Nick had put up to keep the house standing while they replaced some of the structural members. As I rounded the side facing the creek, I noticed that half a dozen of them had snapped. Had the wind been too much for them?

"Were these like this when you got here?" I asked, nudging one of the fallen members with my foot.

"I don't know," he said a little bit sheepishly, and pulled his cap down over his eyes. "I didn't look."

I inspected the other pieces of wood; they were all braced firmly against the house. I was tempted to move the others back into place, but I wasn't sure how to do it, and I didn't want to make a bad situation worse. Was the wet weather or the shifting house responsible for the bracing fail... or, I wondered with a shiver, had someone intentionally sabotaged the braces? It was an unpleasant thing to consider, and I decided to let Ed be the judge of what had happened.

"Well," I said, "I don't know about you, but I could use something cold."

"I could use a Coke," Nick said honestly. "That scared the... well, you know."

"I'll bet," I said. "I don't have Coke, but just picked up a six-pack of ginger beer at the Sweetwater Brewery, if you'd like one," I told him. I'd taken to patronizing the new brewery that had recently started business a mile or two east of the farm. I appreciated their beers, but their non-alcoholic ginger beer was my current favorite summer drink. "I'm not in the mood to pull up more dead plants at the moment, so we might as well take a break while we wait." I glanced up at the sky, which had darkened over the last few minutes: more rain.

"If you're sure, that would be great," he said, following me over to the yellow farmhouse that had once been my grandparents' and now belonged to me.

As Nick sat down on one of the rockers on the porch, I opened the screen door to let my poodle Chuck out and headed inside to grab two ginger beers from the fridge. I also took the liberty of retrieving a jar of my homemade salsa and a bag of salty tortilla chips, which I poured into appropriately sized bowls and set on a tray next to the open bottles. A moment later, Nick and I toasted his survival—and the continued survival of the house—as Chuck sat begging for tortilla chips.

"How long have you been working with Ed?" I asked as I crunched into a chip.

Nick took a swig of ginger ale before answering. "Only a couple of months," he told me. "I... er, didn't do so hot at Texas A&M, so I moved home and my parents made me get a job."

I'd heard that he hadn't had a spectacular debut at college. Then again, many of us hadn't, myself included. I crunched on another chip and reflected that I'd been lucky to have supportive parents who got me some support and gave me a second chance instead of pulling the plug. Nick hadn't been quite as lucky; my friend Molly had told me that his father had refused to pay for any more college after what appeared to have been a challenging first semester.

"It happens," I said. "I don't think I was ready for college yet when I started; my first year was something of a disaster."

"Really?" he asked, perking up.

"It was," I confessed. "Sometimes it's good to take a break and figure things out; I think a job is a great idea."

"Yeah, well, it may be long-term," he said glumly. "I don't see how I can afford to go back."

"Don't worry about that yet," I said. "And when you do, you can look at financial aid if you have to. What do you think of working with Ed?"

"It's hard work," he said. "But it's kind of nice to have something to show for it at the end of the day. I've always liked working with my hands."

Although I was glad Nick was doing something he enjoyed, I hoped Ed was looking over his work; Nick was young and inexperienced, and today's episode did not inspire confidence. I checked my phone to see if I'd missed a call from Ed, and then darted a glance at the little house; thankfully, it didn't seem to have moved any more since we left it.

Nick took another sip from his ginger beer and said, too casually, "Did you happen to see Teena while you were at the brewery?"

"Teena Marburger?" I asked. "No... why?"

"She said she was doing some marketing internship thing for them," he said, shrugging and turning a faint shade of pink. "You know. After school."

"Good for her," I said. "I'll bet she's at the Oktoberfest kickoff tonight, though." Buttercup's week-long Oktoberfest was starting, and the local brewery, which had just opened the past summer, was hosting the opening party and releasing one of the owners' specialty beers. They'd also booked an oompah band, bratwurst and pretzel vendors, and folks making and selling German crafts. I wasn't going to have a booth at the brewery, even though I was going to be selling my wares elsewhere at the festival, but I knew several locals who would be vending their products. "You should go," I suggested.

"Don't you have to be over 21?"

"My friend Molly's bringing her kids," I said. "I think you should be good; you just can't sample the beer, unfortunately." I grinned. "Lots of ginger beer, though. And I think they're making a special 'butter beer.'"

"And pumpkin juice, too?" he asked with a wry smile.

"That always sounded kind of gross to me, honestly," I admitted.

"Me too," he said as Ed's pick-up truck turned into the bottom of the driveway. Nick set his ginger beer down hard —I could tell he was nervous—and practically bolted out of the rocking chair. Together, we hurried to meet Ed as he pulled into the empty space next to my truck.

The back of his white F-150 was filled with spare bits of lumber and a variety of tool chests, and the vehicle was splattered with mud. When he opened the driver's side door, I noticed that he was too.

"Thanks for coming so quickly," I said. "What have you been up to today?"

"Pourin' a foundation on that new house for the Houston folks," he said. "Ran into a few problems; someone trampled the forms, looks like, but I think we got it worked out."

"What about the rain?"

"We covered it with tarps," he said.

"Good thinking. Ginger beer, or iced tea?" I offered.

"No thanks," he said. "I want to see that house."

Together we traipsed across the field to the little old house by the creek.

"What happened?" he asked as we followed him like ducklings trailing a mother duck.

"I was replacing a joist, just like you showed me, and then all of a sudden, the whole house kind of... leaned," Nick said. "When Miz Resnick and I went around the house, we noticed that some of those two-by-fours we used to brace it got knocked over."

"I was wondering if it might be the wind, but I figured you'd know better than I would." I suggested.

"If so, that's the first time that's ever happened on one of my jobs," Ed said gruffly. In addition to his work boots, he wore faded jeans and a plaid shirt that stretched over his round belly. His hair was gray and wiry, and his dark brown eyes were sharp; Nick fidgeted nervously with the hem of his Metallica T-shirt as his boss inspected the cables.

"You're sure you didn't mess with 'em at all?" Ed asked.

"No, sir," Nick said. "I mean, I didn't touch them."

"Did you check 'em before you went in there to work?"

"Ah... no, sir," Nick said, ducking his head.

"Always check," he said. "You were lucky this time. Let it be a lesson to you."

"Yes, sir," Nick replied.

"I don't want anyone going in there until we get this fixed," he said. "You're lucky the whole thing didn't come down on your head."

"That bad?" I asked.

Ed nodded. "That bad." He looked at Nick. "We'll have to brace this again. Might do some on the inside, too, for good measure."

I hugged myself, trying not think about what might have happened to young Nick. "Was it the weather, do you think?"

Ed grimaced. "No weather I've ever seen can snap cables this cleanly."

"You think someone cut them on purpose, then?" I asked.

"I don't like that explanation one bit," Ed said, his voice steely, "but that's what it looks like to me. We're damned lucky Nick here didn't get killed."

2

_E_d and Nick spent the next hour re-bracing the house while I finished shoveling up the dead cucurbit plants. I'd have to rotate crops next year, in hopes that would kill any larvae or eggs that had survived; and I'd probably also have to regularly spray with bT, an organic pesticide that interfered with the growth of the insects, to keep the population in check. As I finished scooping up another mass of dead plants, my eyes strayed to the three beehive frames I was building at the far end of my small peach orchard. It was a good thing bT didn't affect bees, or the sudden infestation would scuttle more than my squash harvest. Serafine Alexandre, who ran the Honeyed Moon meadery and was an expert in bees, had talked me through the beekeeping process and had helped me set up my first few hives. The fledgling colonies were just starting to prosper, and I was hoping to have my own honey and beeswax the following year. The last thing I needed was for a pesticide to knock out my new bee colonies.

I had finished clearing another row of plants when Ed and Nick walked over from the little house.

"All done?" I asked, shielding my eyes from the sun with my hand.

"She'll hold," he said. "We'll do some internal bracing tomorrow, just in case, but I'm worried about vandals. Might want to install a security light down there, just to prevent any more hijinks."

"I probably should have looked for footprints," I said.

"It's a muddy mess now," Ed said. "If it happens again, though..."

"Has anything like this ever happened on any of your other jobs?" I asked.

"Not that I know of," he said. "Of course, there was a contractor who wasn't too happy with me about five years ago. Came back and broke all the windows in a house I was working on, then threw paint all over the darned place."

"No," I said. "Really?"

"Really," he said with a sigh. "Took a week to clean up. But nothing like this." He peered at the house. "Did your goats get into somebody else's vegetable patch one too many times?"

"Not that I know of," I said. Hot Lips and Gidget had made several unchaperoned outings since coming to the farm—including a memorable jaunt to the Christmas Market in downtown Buttercup. As had their buddy Blossom, the cow formerly known as Harriet Houdini, whom I'd acquired from a local dairy farmer who had neglected to inform me of her seemingly magical ability to slip through fences. She was particularly fond of the geraniums that flanked the town hall in the summer time. But I seemed to have finally figured out a fence system that kept them all corralled.

"You never can tell with goats," Ed said ominously. "Heck, they might have chewed through the cables, for all I know."

"I don't think so," I said. "The breaks were clean. Plus, unless they've figured out how to lock gates, there haven't been any recent wanderings."

"I've heard stories," he said. "But I didn't see hoof prints, so they're probably in the clear. Still, it's worrisome. I'd definitely put up a security light; and don't go back in there unless you're sure nothing's been tampered with."

"Got it," I said. "Thanks for coming out to take care of it so quickly."

"We'll be back out tomorrow to do some more work," he said.

"Still on track for spring?"

"That's the plan," he said.

"Terrific. Can I get you a drink?"

"No, ma'am," he said. "Got to get back to that other job. Nick here is just going to finish up a few things and we'll be back tomorrow."

"Thanks again for coming out," I told him.

"Of course," he said, tipping an imaginary hat and giving Nick a few instructions before heading back to his truck.

"Your boss is a good man," I told Nick. "You're lucky."

He gave me a funny look, then dipped his head in something approximating a nod. "I'll just finish up, if that's okay with you, ma'am."

"Of course," I said. "Need another ginger beer?"

"Nah. I'm good," he said.

"I'm probably going to get cleaned up, myself," I said. "I'll see you at the Oktoberfest later on then?"

"Probably," he said with a grin that said "yes," and then headed back to the little house.

I worked for a few more minutes, then gave up and headed in for a shower. A good portion of my harvest might be toast, but at least the little house was still standing, and I had a fun party to go to that night. All in all, not such a bad day after all, I told myself as I stowed the shovel in the shed and walked back up to the farmhouse.

Boy, was I wrong.

WHEN I PULLED up at the Sweetwater Brewery at seven o'clock, the grassy parking area was already full of trucks and cars, and the oaks of the brewery's beer garden were strung with sparkling fairy lights and colorful ribbons. Felix and Simon Gustafson, two brothers, had started the business mere months ago, and I was happy to see it seemed to be thriving. A blue-and-white-checked banner with the words *"Frisch Auf for Oktoberfest"* stretched over the entrance, and the smell of bratwurst and something sweet and fried drifted on the cool breeze. My stomach rumbled as I stepped out of my truck onto the soft (and slightly muddy) grass.

Teena Marburger, the object of Nick's affections, was selling tickets at the gate. She was dressed fetchingly in a dirndl, her long hair braided into a plait that wrapped around her head. Although she was still in high school, she'd had a crush on local farmer Peter Swenson since he'd moved to town in his fry-oil-powered van a couple of years ago and started Green Haven Farm. So far, despite the fact that Peter was dating my best friend Quinn, she seemed undeterred, but I was hoping Nick might be able to persuade her to broaden her horizons. Teena was a good person; she also had an uncanny knack for predicting the future. As I handed over my money, I hoped she wouldn't have any grim prognostications to share today. Fortunately, she seemed to have nothing but a big smile tonight. "Pretty big turnout!" I said. "I'm impressed."

"The PR campaign I tried seemed to work," Teena said excitedly. "I'm so excited about Felix's ideas; he's a genius. He was so smart to use the area's German history and heritage."

"Is that what the *Frisch Auf* is about?" I asked, glancing up at the banner.

"Exactly," she said. "One of the oldest breweries in Texas was located just a few miles from here. It was owned by a German immigrant who brewed the first lager in the area—he called it Bluff Beer. It has to be cool to make it, so he devised this crazy tunnel system to keep it cool enough so he could brew it."

"I had no idea," I said, impressed by her knowledge.

"Of course, there's been a bit of a legal issue with the name," she said, and her face darkened a little.

"What do you mean?"

"Max Pfeiffer is a descendant of the original brewer... it was called Bluff Springs Brewery, and he recently started a new brewery with that name. He's claiming the *'Frisch Auf'* is proprietary, and threatened to sue... but I'm sure that'll get worked out."

"There's always something, isn't there?"

"Isn't that the truth?" she asked.

"You've learned so much. I had no idea beer had such a history in the area."

"I know... me neither! Felix has taught me so much," she said, her eyes sparkling. It looked like Teena might have switched horses from Peter. Beside the fact that Felix was at least a decade her senior, it wasn't looking good for Nick. "Anyway," she continued, "the tradition does come from the original brewery in the area. Every time a new batch of beer was ready, the brewer hung a banner with *Frisch Auf* on it to invite the community to come and celebrate. Since we recently launched an updated version of the original Bluff Springs lager, we decided to bring back the banner. We're even going to use local barley, just like he did!"

"There's local barley now?" I asked. Clearly I was behind the times.

"Oh, yes," she said. "Adriana Janacek grew the first batch last winter, although it didn't work out too well." She made a face, then brightened. "Anyway, I hear Peter's going to try experimenting with growing some this coming season." Her eyes did still sparkle a bit when she mentioned the young farmer's name, and I stifled a sigh, but Teena didn't seem to notice. "We've got local wines in Texas—at least in the Hill Country, and out in West Texas, but until now, we haven't had true local beer. Ours is one of the first to source most of its products locally. There's even a farmer in Round Top who's starting to grow hops hydroponically!"

"Huh," I said. "Maybe I should check that out. I don't have hydroponic equipment, but I could try a few plants this fall. They're perennials, so it may take a while for them to produce, but it's worth a shot."

"I'll get you her name if you want to talk to her," Teena said, pulling out her cell phone. "I'll text you her contact."

"Wow. Thanks. You really have a passion for this stuff, Teena. And you're good at it, too!"

"Thanks," she said with a grin. "I'm definitely going to see if I can go to school to study communications; it's so much fun!"

"Maybe you can help me out at the farm next summer," I said.

"Sure! Do you have a web site or any social media presence?" she asked.

I'd started a Twitter account a few years back, and I'd heard that an online presence was important for small businesses, but updating my web site and Twitter had dropped to the bottom of the list of chores. In fact, if I was being honest, it had completely fallen off the list of chores. "Not much of one," I admitted, feeling sheepish. "To be honest, I really could use some help."

"I'd be happy to do that," she said. "As long as you can wait till June!"

"I've waited this long," I said with a grin and more than a little bit of relief that I'd be off the hook for while yet. "But you just graduated, didn't you?"

She nodded excitedly. "I'm taking a year off to do this internship. I'm already looking at programs at UT and A&M."

"That's terrific," I said. As I spoke, a young man I didn't recognize came up behind Teena and put his hands on her bare shoulders. She flinched a little, but he didn't move his hands. He was good-looking, probably in his early twenties, a bit burly, with a tattoo of a wolf on his neck.

"Hey, beautiful," he said. "I've been looking for you."

"Hi, Billy," she said, her smile gone.

"Who's this?" he asked, fixing me with sharp brown eyes.

"I'm Lucy Resnick," I said, proffering a hand. He shook it hard, squeezing so much that my knuckles hurt.

"I'm Billy Brindle," he said. "I'm one of the brewers here."

"I thought that was Felix's department," I said.

"Too much for one person," he said with a self-satisfied smile. "And I'm teaching him a few tricks, too," he added, puffing himself up a little bit. Teena rolled her eyes and pulled away; as she did, I noticed Nick about ten yards away, watching the whole thing with a scowl on his face. Something about the way he was watching Teena was unsettling; there was a menacing look in his eyes that unnerved me.

"I think Felix was looking for you a few minutes ago," Teena said in a clipped voice, distracting me from Nick.

"Really? What did he want?"

"I don't know, but you might want to go find him," she suggested.

"You're just playing hard to get, aren't you?" he asked in a voice that made my skin crawl. "You should try hanging out with someone your own age sometime. I think you'll like it."

"Leave me alone," she said in a firm voice, shrugging him off and stepping away.

"What?" he asked, blinking innocently. "I'm just playing around."

I felt the urge to punch the cocky young man, who clearly couldn't take no for an answer.

"We're done here," she said. "Goodbye."

"You don't have to be such a goody two-shoes, you know," he said in a hurt voice. "I'll let you play hard to get, for now. But I'll see you around." He paused, and then, in a silky but menacing tone, added, "Promise."

With that veiled threat still dangling in the air, he swaggered away. Nick had melted into the crowd, but something told me he'd seen what had happened.

"He's a real creep," I told Teena.

"I know," she said, looking miserable, "but Felix says he's talented. So I put up with it."

"You shouldn't have to," I said.

She sighed and looked away; I could tell she was uncomfortable, so I changed topics—for now, anyway. "Hey... by the way, have you seen Dr. Brandt?" I asked. Tobias Brandt was Buttercup's resident vet; we'd been seeing each other since not long after I moved to town. He'd told me he'd meet me after he finished with his calls, and I'd hoped he'd gotten done early.

"Not yet," she said, shaking her head.

"Ah, well. I'll just have to start without him, won't I?"

"I suppose I should take your money and let you in," Teena said. "They're doing the special Dubbel Trouble tasting in a bit; it's Felix's pride and joy. They're tapping the first keg in an hour."

"Thanks for the tip," I said as she took my money and stamped the back of my hand.

"Have fun!" she told me.

"You too." I grinned as I drifted into the throng of the Oktoberfest opening celebration.

It smelled amazing... not just like beer, but also bratwurst sizzling over a brazier, and candied almonds from a stall near the beer tent. Several local craftsmen had booths with beautiful objects in wood and pottery, along with a few early Christmas ornaments I did my best to ignore. Serafine Alexandre was there, too, offering bottles of mead for those who weren't keen on beer; I was happy to see that the Gustafson brothers had extended an invitation to the meadery, whose product could have been viewed as competition. I was surprised to see short, stout Max Pfeiffer at the bratwurst booth, if there was bad blood between Max and the Gustafsons. I was thankful I didn't have that kind of relationship with the local farmers; we all helped each other out instead of tearing each other down.

I'd chosen to dress casually, in jeans and a long-sleeved T-shirt, but a lot of the folks with German heritage—and some who just liked to dress up—had gone all out for the occasion. I wasn't surprised to see Flora Kocurek dressed in a dirndl; she'd recently discovered her heritage was not just Czech, as she'd grown up thinking, but also included a hefty dose of German. Based on the fluffy green skirt and bodice, she had evidently embraced this new part of herself. Her boyfriend, Gus, was rather more restrained in his typical white button-down shirt, jeans, and boots; his only concession to the festivities was a blue and white button on his shirt pocket, which I had no doubt had been put there by Flora.

"Lucy!" Flora beamed when she spotted me. "Where's Tobias?"

"He's not here yet," I said. "I like your outfit!"

"Thank you," she said. "I tried to get Gus here interested in a pair of Lederhosen, but..."

"Nothin' doin'," he said succinctly, but he looked at Flora fondly. "She does turn out nice, though, doesn't she?"

"She does," I agreed. Since she'd lost her domineering mother a while back, after fifty-plus years of being under Nettie Kocurek's thumb, Flora had slowly been coming into her own. It was a delight to watch her blossom, and she was looking happier every day. Since Opal Gruber down at the sheriff's office had been giving her some tips on make-up, she'd toned down the bright red lipstick and pancake make-up for a more subtle color palette that made her glow. I could see why Gus was enamored. I glanced down at the beer mug in Flora's hand. "What are you drinking?"

"The Bluff lager," she said. "Gus likes the oatmeal stout, but it's kind of heavy for me; I prefer the lager. It's really good with the bratwurst; you should get some!"

"I will in a minute," I said. "Did you try the candied almonds?"

"They're to die for," Flora confessed. As she spoke, Molly and Alfie strolled up; Molly was carrying a paper cone of almonds, and Alfie had a giant glass mug of beer.

"You made it!" Molly said, grinning, as I hugged both of them.

"I did," I said, "but I haven't had a chance to get a beer yet."

"Well, let's fix that," she said. "I could use something to wet my whistle, too." Molly smiled at Flora. "Mind if I steal Lucy away for a minute?"

"No problem," Gus said. "Line's short right now; best go get one while you can!"

As Molly and I headed over to the beer tent, she said, "I was hoping I could get you alone for a few minutes."

"What's wrong?" I asked.

"I have a bad feeling about tonight," she said. "I ran into Max Pfeiffer and Felix at the Red & White yesterday—I was down picking up some ground beef for chili—and Max and Felix were having a massive argument by the ice cream freezer."

"I heard there was some kind of lawsuit," I said.

"It sounds like more than a lawsuit," she said. "I've never seen Max so angry. He told Felix if he didn't close up shop and move out of Buttercup, he'd run him out of town himself."

"Felix and Simon seem to have been pretty successful," I said, looking around at the crowded festival. "They've done a much better job of promoting themselves than Max Pfeiffer has."

"Well, he's suing the Gustafsons for using '*Frisch Auf*' and the 'Bluff' name. Those started with the Pfeiffer Brewery back in the 1800s, so he may have a case," she said.

"Sounds like it," I said. "Felix and Simon have done such a good job with the brewery, though, that I'll bet they'll get a good attorney and take care of things quickly."

"I hope so," she said.

"They've made a lot of this place in such a short time, haven't they?"

"Hard to believe that only two years ago this was a falling-down barn," I said, looking over at the freshly painted barn adorned with lights. The brothers had completely renovated it into a tasting room/brew pub, and turned the adjoining grove of live oaks into a beautiful beer garden, with swaths of fragrant rosemary, purple sage, yellow bells, and even a few vegetables tucked in here and there, including some beautiful butternut squash that had escaped the scourge of the melon worm. I was a little bit jealous.

"I just hope Max doesn't scuttle it," Molly said.

As she spoke, over the thrum of conversations and the oompah band that was warming up on the stage at the far end of the beer garden I heard raised voices.

"I told you I don't want him here," one voice said.

"I can't control who comes or who doesn't," the other voice responded.

"Maybe not, but you sure didn't have to invite him. I told you; I don't want anything to do with that outfit."

Molly and I glanced at each other; wordlessly, we edged closer to the argument. Whoever it was, they were standing behind a big rosemary bush by the corner of the barn. I peered through the branches: it was Simon and Felix Gustafson.

"It's good business," said Simon. The two brothers were about the same height and close in age, but other than that, the only thing they had in common was that they wore beards.

"It's selling out is what it is," Felix replied. He wore baggy jeans, a big Texas belt buckle, muddy boots, and a plaid flannel shirt that looked like it had been around at least as long as Felix himself. The general effect was Grizzly Adams Goes to Texas.

Simon, on the other hand, wore a blue button-down, shiny brown loafers, and khakis with creases you could cut yourself on. And while Felix's beard looked like it could comfortably house a family of wrens, Simon's was neatly trimmed... almost vestigial, in fact. I wondered if the only reason he wasn't completely clean-shaven was that facial hair appeared to be a basic requirement for craft brewers... at least in my (admittedly limited) experience. "It's good business," he repeated. "We've had a good run, but if we want to grow, we need access to distributors to help get us on grocery store shelves."

"Why do we need to be on grocery store shelves?" Felix asked. "I don't want to be the next Budweiser. I thought when we went into this we agreed we'd stay true to our roots."

"We are staying true to our roots," Simon said. "We're just... joining up with other craft brewers. It'll help us."

"I don't want to make other people's beers," Felix said. "I want to make our beer."

"And we will!" Simon reassured him. "With more capital and better distribution, we'll get to expand. You can experiment all you like with new techniques. We can help invest in local products... like the barley we ordered from Adriana."

"Which was a total bust."

"This time," Simon said.

"This time? I heard her threaten you this morning. She says we bankrupted her."

"She'll bounce back," Simon said in a soothing voice. "I've been talking with her. It'll come around. I promise you."

"I know you think so," Felix said, "but you're wrong. And you can't do this without me."

There was an ominous silence before he continued. "I knew it was trouble to do the Bluff Lager, and to use the *Frisch Auf* banner, and now we're being sued. I saw him a few minutes ago, badmouthing us to a group of people by the bratwurst stand." He ran a hand through his hair. "I gave in on that, and look what happened? I won't give in on this."

"Felix..."

"That's my final word. Sweetwater will become a part of Brewlific over my dead body."

3

"*Well*, that was certainly interesting," Molly murmured after Felix stormed off.

"I didn't realize they were at such odds," I said, watching as Simon headed over and shook hands with a woman I didn't recognize. Her khaki slacks and blazer seemed out of place in the casual setting, and I wondered if she might be connected to whatever Brewlific was. "Business seems to be booming," I told Molly as I watched Simon chatting with the woman, a salesy smile on his face. "I just assumed that they were on the same page about running it."

"Doesn't seem that way at all," Molly replied, biting her lip and looking concerned. "They really seemed like they were at an impasse."

"I'm sure they'll figure it out," I said, although I hoped I was right.

"What's Brewlific, anyway?" Molly asked.

"I don't know, but it sounds like Simon doesn't want the brewery to be quite as independent anymore." I'd never considered it, but I could see the benefit of banding with other farmers... that way, not all of us would lose our cucurbit crops to melon worms at the same time.

"Let's hope they work it out," Molly said doubtfully. As she spoke, the loudspeaker crackled.

"The first tasting of our special recipe seasonal brew, Dubbel Trouble, will start in five minutes in the beer tent."

I looked at Molly. "Dubbel Trouble, eh?"

"Aptly named," she grimaced. Together, we walked over to the tent, where a line was already forming.

"What is it, anyway?" I asked.

"Whatever it is, it looks like it's in barrels," she said.

"Oh, it is," said a familiar voice at my elbow. I turned to see one of my favorite people, looking handsome in jeans, boots, and an "Everybody's Somebody in Luckenbach" T-shirt stretched over a chest that (to my eye) had benefited greatly from the strenuous life of a country vet.

"Tobias!" I said, as my heart picked up the pace a few notches. He enveloped me in a hug and kissed me lightly before turning to greet Molly, who, although happily married to Alfie Kramer, seemed a little wistful as she smiled at him.

"So, what do you know about Dubbel Trouble?" she asked teasingly.

"It's aged in whiskey barrels," he said. "Dubbel is a Belgian-style beer; that's why it's spelled Dubbel, D-u-b-b-e-l, not Double as in two of something. It should be good; I'm looking forward to trying it."

"I'm not sure I've had Belgian-style beer," Molly said.

"Me neither," I added.

"Well, I'm sure this one will be good," Tobias said. "Felix really knows what he's doing."

"I hope they don't run out," I said. "There's only one barrel, and that's an awfully long line."

"I'm sure they have more in the back," he said as Felix stepped up to the barrel. At some point, someone had put a tap in it.

"Thanks so much for coming out for our tasting of Dubbel Trouble," Felix said into the cordless microphone in his hand. "As I'm sure many of you know, Dubbel beer was first brewed by Trappist monks in Westmalle Abbey in Belgium in 1856. It's a dark-brown beer with a lovely, deep flavor...you'll taste raisins, prunes, and dates. In fact, I like to think of it as a drinkable, alcoholic sticky toffee pudding," He flashed his teeth in what I presumed was a grin. It was hard to tell through the facial shrubbery. "We achieved the deep flavor with caramelized beet sugar, special yeast, and a few delicate spices. We then went the extra step and aged our special brew in whiskey barrels to accentuate that autumn flavor."

Mandy Vargas from the *Buttercup Zephyr* was a few feet to the side, taking notes, and a young woman in a Sweetwater Brewery T-shirt, was busy snapping pictures as he spoke. I looked for Simon; he was over in the corner of the tent with the woman I'd seen him talking with earlier; they were deep in conversation. Felix noticed him, too. "If my brother would be kind enough to come join me, we'll toast the first taste of Sweetwater's special seasonal brew."

Simon beamed, excusing himself from his conversation, and strode to the makeshift wooden stage where his brother stood beside the barrel.

"Ready?" Felix asked as his brother arrived.

"Ready," Simon said, taking the microphone as Felix reached for a small glass from a table to the right of the barrel. "Thanks so much for coming out to our Oktoberfest opening celebration. We're so grateful to Buttercup for being such a big part of our success... we hope to have more big news to share soon!"

As he spoke, Felix's head jerked around, and his eyebrows drew down into a frown. "This is supposed to be about the beer!" he hissed.

"It's always about the beer," Simon replied, his rather sales-y smile not faltering. Molly and I exchanged glances.

Felix muttered something inaudible in response and put the first glass under the tap. Dubbel Trouble looked delicious, I had to admit; it was a dark, rich brown that glowed in the lights, with a creamy head that was the color of browned butter. I wasn't usually much of a beer drinker, but after that delightful description, my mouth was watering as Felix handed the first glass to his brother and poured another for himself.

The photographer was snapping pictures in a frenzy as Felix and Simon raised their beers for a toast. "*Prosit!*" Felix said as the glasses clinked, and as they raised them to their lips, the whole tent burst into applause.

A moment later, both men were spewing beer onto the wooden stage.

"What did you do to my beer?" Felix barked at his brother, looking like a wounded child.

"I didn't do anything to it," Simon shot back, then recovered himself. "Sorry, folks. Must have been a problem with the barrel. We'll get another one up here and tap it..."

"I tested it earlier though," Felix said. "Someone must have done something to it."

"We'll talk about it later," Simon interjected. "Let's get this one out of here and get a new one, shall we? Sorry about this, folks; it happens sometimes! Just usually not on stage!" His apologetic tone won him a few chuckles.

There was a flurry of activity as a few employees rolled the offending barrel away. A few minutes later, two young men in blue shirts—one of whom I recognized as the offensive Billy—carried in another one.

"Let's hope we have better luck with this one, eh?" Simon said lightly as his brother set about tapping the new barrel, this time taking a small sip before doing anything further. "All good?" Simon asked.

"All good," his brother replied. A moment later, they repeated the toast to scattered applause, but the line had diminished, and the enthusiasm was definitely lower than it had been. I glanced over to where I'd seen the blazer-clad woman chatting with Simon before the ill-fated toast, but she was gone.

"Folks, we're going to go check on the other barrels now, but please, enjoy some Dubbel Trouble... and thanks so much for coming!" More scattered applause, and then the two men exited the back of the tent, Simon staring at his phone with a brittle smile, and Felix talking to him in what looked like a very emphatic manner. I could only imagine that the barrel issue had thrown fuel on the fire. I wondered what had happened to the beer. If the second barrel was okay, it must have been a problem with just that barrel.

"Do you think it was just a bad barrel?" Tobias asked, echoing my thoughts as we walked over to the line.

"I don't know," I said. "I'm wondering if someone tampered with it."

"Why would they do that?" Molly asked.

I shrugged. "I know someone who would."

Tobias gave me a sharp look. "Who?"

"Max Pfeiffer, for one," I suggested. "I heard he was here today."

"Oh, Max." Tobias grimaced. "He opened that tiny brewery a couple of years ago off SH 71, didn't he? I tried his beer once. It was like... well..."

"Yellow water?" I supplied.

"Exactly," Tobias concurred. "Only with a little bit of fizz."

"You're selling it hard, my friend," Molly said.

"Well," Tobias said, "it's not exactly something you want to buy by the keg. Anyway, there was some rumor about a lawsuit."

"That's what Teena and Molly were just telling me. That Max is angry about all the buzz they're getting, trading on his family's ideas."

"Well, then, he should have thought about that when he opened his own brewery," Tobias said.

"I guess by the time he did think of it, it was too late."

"Sour grapes," Molly said.

"Or sour beer," said Bubba Allen, who was standing just next to us in line.

"Hey, Bubba!" I said, turning to the tall, stocky man. Bubba ran Bubba's Barbecue, which had terrific sausage, including venison sausage made to order for local hunters. He had a few recipes his grandparents had brought over when they emigrated from Bamberg, Germany, and he made the best bratwurst I'd had on this side of the Atlantic. It was definitely on the menu for tonight. "Taking a break from the bratwurst to grab a beer?"

"Felix has been going on about this new Dubbel for a month now," he said. "I got someone to cover the booth for a few while I sample it. At least that bad first barrel shortened the line some."

"What do you think it was?"

"I don't know," Bubba said. "But it's not like Felix. He

always samples things in advance. If they were all like that, I'd think it was something wrong with the whole batch, although he's such a chemist he would have picked up on that long before today."

"I'm sure he samples along the way, too."

Bubba nodded. "I always fry up a little bit before I finish mixing up the sausage, just in case. My bet is that someone tampered with that barrel to make them look bad, what with the paper bein' here and all." He lowered his voice. "And I'd put my money on Max Pfeiffer."

"Is he still here?"

"I saw him earlier," he said, "talking to someone about how the brewery 'stole' his name."

"Since he was here, he must have had an opportunity to mess with the barrel," I said.

"You ain't wrong," Bubba said.

"How well do you know Felix and Simon?" I asked.

"Oh, they talked to me a bit before they set up shop in town, askin' for business advice. I told 'em what I could, but brewin's a different business from makin' sausage. They're good boys, though. Hard-workin'."

"I get the feeling they have different views of where they want to take things," I said.

"Isn't that normal for family? Don't always agree on everything, but they manage to make it work." As he spoke, we reached the front of the line, and a young man poured him a glass of dark Dubbel Trouble, with a creamy head.

"Thank you kindly, sir," Bubba said, and tipped his hat to us. "Nice talkin' to you, but I got to get back to work."

"We'll see you there shortly," I said. A moment later, one of the brewery employees handed me a glass of Dubbel Trouble, and I took an appreciative sip before moving out of the way. It did taste a little like a liquid sticky toffee pudding, and it was absolutely delicious. I was glad they only made it for special occasions, or I'd probably drink far too much of it. I took a few more sips, and a few minutes later, Tobias, Molly and I drifted out of the tent, all with full glasses in hand.

"Ready to get a bratwurst?" Tobias asked.

"Absolutely," I said. "And then I want to take the brewery tour."

"I should probably go find Alfie," Molly said. "And I need to make sure the kids eat something other than funnel cake."

"There's funnel cake?" I asked.

Tobias laughed. "There's funnel cake. And ice cream, and bratwurst, and Quinn's got some lebkuchen at the Blue Onion booth..."

"Lebkuchen?" Lebkuchen was a kind of German gingerbread that was soft and often dipped in chocolate; my mouth watered just thinking about it. "I love that stuff."

"Well, she's got a bunch of it. Plus pretzels, and even some Texas Sheet Cake."

"I wish you hadn't told me. Now I'm going to have to sample all of them."

"We've got plenty of time," Tobias said. "Let's go get some dinner, and then we'll check out the brewery."

We spent the next twenty minutes strolling through the beer garden, chatting with friends and admiring the offerings at the artisans' booths. I was sorely tempted by a beautiful cream pitcher with hand-painted blue flowers that I knew would look beautiful in my kitchen, but decided against it; money was still tight on my fledgling farm.

Whether Sweetwater signed on with Brewlific or not,

they seemed to be doing a booming business. The beer was flowing copiously, along with the root beer and ginger beer, and it seemed that half of not just Buttercup, but a good portion of Austin and Houston had showed up for the event. The weather, fortunately, had cooperated; despite the moist heat we'd had recently, it was a cooler day, and I could feel just a hint of fall in the air. The band was taking a break, but two older couples in dirndls and lederhosen were doing the polka to piped oompah music, to the applause of onlookers. I grinned; they looked happy. I hoped Tobias and I would be like that in a few decades. I glanced up at my handsome boyfriend. What was he thinking for the future? I wondered, as I had increasingly lately. We hadn't really discussed where we were going with things, and I was starting to think about it more and more. Would I want to live in the same house with someone else? I enjoyed my independence, but it was nice to wake up next to someone, too... particularly someone like Tobias. Did I want to get married? Did Tobias? And what about kids?

I bit into a bratwurst and took another swig of beer, banishing those thoughts from my head. I was eyeing the funnel cakes when they announced the brewery tour over the loudspeaker.

"Funnel cake, or tour?" Tobias asked, tearing off a piece of pretzel.

"I don't want to get powdered sugar all over the brewery," I said, although I wanted a funnel cake more than just about anything.

"Let's do the tour, and then we'll get funnel cake. And ice cream."

"It's a deal," I said, and together we headed over to the tent where the beer tasting had been.

There was a bit of confusion when we arrived. "Have you seen Felix anywhere?" asked Teena, who had moved from the front gate to the tour section. "He was supposed to do the opening talk." Nick was nearby, I noticed, looking at Teena with barely veiled longing. To which she appeared completely oblivious. I would have loved to encourage him, but I was beginning to think it might be a hopeless cause.

"Last time I saw him was at the Dubbel Trouble tapping," replied Billy, who—predictably—couldn't seem to leave Teena alone. "I told him we should have checked that barrel right before the tasting, but he wouldn't listen. Good thing I've got copies of his recipes now; he's so disorganized he'll probably lose them. Must be old age."

Teena checked her phone, ignoring Billy's prattle and leering stare. "The tour's supposed to start in two minutes; what do I do?"

"Don't be a wuss," Billy said. "I thought you were a big, strong woman."

Teena looked up, and a shadow crossed her face. "Oh, no," she said.

I hurried up to her, my stomach clenching. Teena had a pretty good track record when it came to premonitions, and I had a feeling this was one of them.

"What's going on?" I asked, inserting myself between her and Billy. "Are you okay?"

"I just... I don't want to go in there," she said, looking at the big double doors that led to the working part of the brewery.

"What's the big deal?" Billy said. "It's time. I'm going to start the tour." Without consulting her further, he pushed open the double doors. I was still watching Teena, who had turned white; around me, the crowd gasped. A second later, Teena turned and screamed, then crumpled to the floor. I turned to look at what everyone else was seeing, and my stomach dropped.

Felix Gustafson —or what I could see of him—was lying on the concrete floor, in a pool of what appeared to be blood. On top of him was a gigantic white bag, with something that looked like barley spilling out the top.

4

                 ———

*T*obias dropped his pretzel and ran over to Felix. He tried to push the giant bag off of him, but it was too heavy. I ran to join him, as did about four men, including Alfie Kramer; together, we managed to shift it enough so that it was no longer crushing him. As I stepped away, I accidentally kicked a red and white beer can that had been spilled a few feet from the body.

"I'm calling 911," I said, dialing the number as Tobias crouched beside the burly brewer. A moment later he was joined by Linda Fernandez, who I knew was a nurse. She felt for Felix's pulse while Tobias inspected the damage. After only a few seconds, they exchanged looks, and I could tell by their grim faces that any ambulance would be too late.

As I relayed information to the dispatcher, I hurried over to Teena, who was sprawled on the ground. Simon was standing nearby white-faced and apparently incapacitated. As I took her wrist to check her pulse, Nick appeared beside me, alarm written on his chiseled features. "Is she okay?"

Linda hurried over to us as he spoke. "I'm going to defer

to the expert," I told him, nodding toward Linda. She checked Teena's breathing and pulse, then opened the girl's mouth to make sure she wasn't choking on anything. "She's going to have a goose egg, I think," she said, "but her vitals look good from what I can see. I can't get blood pressure, but pulse and respiration are okay. I'm guessing she just fainted, but I can't be sure."

"I told the dispatcher we'd need paramedics," I said. "What should we do for now?"

"Do we have anything we can use to elevate her feet a bit?" she asked. I handed over my bag, and she placed it under Teena's small feet. "We need to keep her from moving if we can," she said. "Let's just monitor her till they get here."

As she spoke, Teena's eyelids twitched. "It's repeating," she murmured, and opened her eyes.

"Just stay put, darlin'," Linda said in a soothing voice. "We're here with you."

"The history. It's repeating itself..."

"Just worry about you right now," she said in a soothing voice. She was about to say something else when a loud, instantly recognizable voice boomed out behind us.

"What's all this about a dead body? Opal just called sayin' somethin' about someone gettin' crushed under a load of grain?"

Teena let out a low moan and attempted to crane her head to see. Linda glared at Rooster Kocurek, our local sheriff, who was waddling up to the crime scene with a huge mug of beer in one hand and a bratwurst in the other. He was evidently off-duty, as he wore a bright orange 'Gone Fishin'' T-shirt stretched over his ample girth, paired with khaki cargo shorts that looked like they were straining at the seams. "What's goin' on here?" he asked as Linda moved to position herself between Teena and Felix's body and again told Teena not to move.

"Let's close these doors," Tobias suggested, just as Simon stumbled up to the front of the brewery, looking shocked. "Felix," he said. "Where's Felix?"

I exchanged glances with Linda, then stood up and hurried over to Simon. His eyes fixed on his brother as I reached him. The blood drained from his face, and his mouth went slack. "No..."

I took his arm and tried to turn him away, but he was rooted to the spot. "Is he..."

"I'm afraid so," I said. "Come on. Let's find somewhere to sit down..."

"No," he said. "No!" Before I could stop him, he wrenched free and ran over to his brother, pretty much throwing himself across him. "He can't be gone. Can't be." He stood up and looked around wildly. "Who did this? Who?" He ran a hand through his short hair, then said, "Max. It must have been Max Pfeiffer. Jealous of our success. He wanted the name back, so he figured..."

"Don't you worry 'bout who did in your brother," Rooster said, hitching up his cargo shorts. "You leave that to the police."

Simon blinked at Rooster. "You mean you?" he asked.

"I'm the sheriff of Fayette County," Rooster said, his reddish wattle jiggling as he nodded.

"You've got to be kidding me," Simon said, voicing what just about everybody I knew had thought at one time or another. "Aren't you the idiot who shot himself in the foot?"

As he spoke, Rooster's wife Lacey appeared, looking harried. She was a bright-eyed woman with dark hair and (rumor had it) an increasingly limited supply of patience with her dullard husband. She'd kicked him out a while back, and although they were together again, I'd heard a rumor that some of the locals were running a pool on how long it would be before she showed him the door again.

Evidently she hadn't heard what Simon said, because she launched right into what she had to say. "Rooster, you're supposed to be off-duty today, remember? We're all waitin' for you."

"I'm a little busy here, darlin'," he said, the words laced with sarcasm. He was staring at Simon with narrowed eyes... he didn't even turn to glance at his wife.

"You're always busy," she complained. "The kids want funnel cake..." She broke off mid-sentence when she saw Felix lying on the ground. Her hands went to her face. "Oh. Oh, my," she breathed, then turned and plunged back into the crowd.

Once Lacey had disappeared, Rooster stalked toward Simon, something about his gait reminding me of a little boy trying to be John Wayne. He stopped about just in front of him, rocking up on his toes to give him height (he still fell short by about six inches) and shoved a chubby finger in the younger man's face. "You watch yourself, boy," he hissed. "I'll give you a pass this time, since you're new in town, but one more word outta you..."

"Sheriff Kocurek," Tobias said in a warning voice. Tobias's father had been a cop, and a good one. "That sounds almost like a threat."

Rooster's head swiveled, and his beady eyes fixed on Tobias. The portly sheriff opened his mouth to say something, then evidently reconsidered. Instead, he turned back to Simon and jabbed a finger at the body. "That over there was your brother."

The soul of sensitivity, I thought, cringing. Poor Simon.

Simon nodded, his handsome face the color of milk, and

turned away from his brother's remains, as if he couldn't bear to look at them. I totally understood. I wasn't even related to the man, and I couldn't bear to look at them, either.

"I hear you two had a dust-up earlier today," Rooster said in a low, menacing voice. "You might start thinkin' about where you've been the past few hours, and who can vouch for you. I don't mind sayin', right now it doesn't look too good for you."

Simon swallowed. Rooster might be a bad cop, but he wasn't wrong, and Simon grasped that immediately. "I would never harm my brother," he said in a tight, calm voice, the earlier near-hysteria now completely under control. "We loved each other."

"Don't mix business and family, isn't that the sayin'?" Rooster said. Then he rocked back on his heels and smirked. "Maybe you shoulda listened."

Simon took a step back, looking as if Rooster had slapped him. Then he seemed to pull himself together. "I'm happy to answer any questions you have, but this is a crime scene. Shouldn't you be doing something to secure it?"

Rooster made a sour face, looking like he'd bitten into an overcured dill pickle.

"Everybody step back," he said. "I'm closin' these doors. But y'all don't go anywhere; I've got questions to ask."

"All of us?" asked a woman a little behind him, who had been watching the proceedings wide-eyed. "How are you going to do that?"

"Just... just don't go home until we tell you," he said lamely, and then busied himself on his phone.

"Are you okay?" I asked Simon in a low voice. He was staring at the closed double doors, looking haunted.

"No," he said. "I just... we've been together our whole

lives." He turned to me. "What am I going to do now that he's gone?"

"It'll be okay," I reassured him. "Let's go get you a drink of water, get you inside where it's quieter." As I spoke, the wail of sirens pierced the air. I glanced over at Teena.

"It's repeating," she said, quite loudly. Then she closed her eyes again.

"Does she have a history of seizures?" Linda asked me quietly.

"Not that I know of," I said. "We might want to get in touch with her parents, though. I've got their number on my phone; I'll give them a call in a minute."

"Thanks," she said. "I'm sure they'll want to know."

As I walked Simon over to the main office building, which was a Texas-style farmhouse with a long, wide porch a ways back from the brewhouse, he started rambling again. "I've got to find out who did this. I thought we were past everything, and now this. What will I tell Mother?"

"Past everything?" I asked as we stepped up onto the porch. "How so?"

He jerked his head around. "Did I say that? I just meant... all that work to get this place going," he said hurriedly. "Getting the loan, figuring out the distribution, doing the marketing... this dream took a lot of hard work."

"I understand," I said. "I struggle with some of the same things myself. Can I go in and get you that glass of water?"

"No... I'm fine," he said, looking anything but. "I'm... I'm just going to sit down for a minute. Then I've got to make sure everything's going okay... since I'm now the only one running the place." He looked miserable.

"Are you sure?"

"I'm sure," he said. "This whole thing has been a disaster."

"The festival is going really well," I countered. "It's just there was a terrible accident."

"Accident?" he said, looking at me. "That's not what Rooster thinks. And he thinks I'm the one who killed my own brother."

I couldn't argue with him. "It'll all work out, I'm sure," I reassured him, although I did wonder. Felix had evidently been standing in the way of Simon expanding the business.

"Right," he said, shrugging me off. "I've got to go make sure things are progressing," he said. "Thanks for the help... now, if you'll excuse me..."

"Of course," I said, and watched him hurry across the field toward the festival tents. As I stood on the porch, I noticed a stack of envelopes on a table by the door. The top one was addressed to the brewery. "NOTICE OF LATE PAYMENT." It was from a mortgage company.

I thought about the argument I'd overheard between Simon and his brother earlier in the day. Felix was against growing the business... but it looked like growing the business might the only choice the brothers had had if they wanted to keep the brewery.

Had Simon been desperate enough to avoid bankruptcy that he'd eliminated the only thing standing in his way?

Even if it was his own brother?

5

*T*he tragedy had put a damper on the festive air, but there was plenty of gossip floating around the festival grounds as I walked through them looking for Quinn's booth. Even with the oompah band playing, I could still hear what people were saying. I'd called Teena's parents, but gotten voicemails both times; I'd asked them to call me as soon as possible, and made sure my ringer was on. Now, I was keeping an ear out for what the locals thought of the situation.

"I heard it was a forklift," one woman said as she walked by me, her mouth half full of bratwurst.

"He was in the beer barrel when they opened it," another said.

"I heard it was a skeleton in his closet that came back to haunt him," someone else commented. By the time I found Quinn counting out squares of bee-sting cake and boxing up gingerbread hearts for her customers, I'd heard at least a half a dozen accounts of how Felix had died. None of them were correct.

"Oh my gosh!" Quinn said as she finished doling out another two of the honey-and-cream-laced bee-sting—or Bienenstich, as they were known in German—squares to hungry customers. "Everyone's flocking over here for comfort food after what happened. I hear Felix keeled over with a knife in his back and Teena had some kind of epileptic fit!"

"Not exactly," I said.

"What happened, then?" she asked, taking off her gloves and handing over the reins to one of her helpers for a few minutes.

I gave her the rundown on what had happened, including Rooster's comments.

"So Rooster's already decided Simon is guilty."

"Honestly, he has a point. He and Felix did have an argument earlier today," I said. "And I think the brewery may be in some financial straits." I told her what I'd found on the porch of the house.

"Ouch," she said. "Starting up a business is expensive. I'll bet Simon was banking on that distributorship to get things rolling. I wonder if the deal is scuttled after today? I mean, first that bad barrel of beer at the reveal, and now this..."

"It's not good," she said. "And I know at least three reporters were here to do coverage; one of the TV stations was supposed to come out, too."

"Well, they'll certainly be getting publicity."

"But not quite the kind they were looking for, I'm afraid," Quinn said. "On the plus side, it's been good for the comfort food trade. Speaking of which, do you think Bubba has any more bratwurst?"

"Let's go check," I said. "I could use another one myself."

"And a glass of that Bluff lager," she said. "That stuff is just delicious."

"I know. They make great beer, don't they?" I wasn't much of a beer drinker, but Simon and Felix had some kind of brewing magic; their stuff was amazing.

"They've been trying to make it with local barley," she said.

"I heard that. And I also heard it didn't work out."

"Well, there was a bit of a brouhaha—no pun intended—with Adriana Janacek not too long ago." Adriana, I knew, came from a local farming family and had land a bit north of town. "She contracted with the brewery to grow a crop of barley and sell it to them."

"Someone said something about it not working out, and Adriana being bankrupted?"

"Maybe not bankrupted," Quinn said, "but not in great shape. It turns out the barley wasn't up to snuff. The brewery wouldn't buy it, so Adriana had to sell it for animal feed. She only got pennies on the dollars they expected."

"Ouch," I said, wincing.

"Yeah. She dedicated three-quarters of the farm to the barley crop."

"That's a big risk," I said.

"And a bad one. I heard she was talking about suing the brewery for breach of contract."

"Everyone's talking about lawsuits, it seems. But if the crop was spoiled, the brewery would be paying for something they couldn't use," I pointed out, and let out a sigh. "That's the trouble with farming. Last week my squash and melon crops looked like something out of *Modern Farmer* Now the whole field looks like a worm farm."

"Oh, no," Quinn said. "Are you going to be okay?"

"It's a hit, but that's why I diversify," I said with a shrug. "The peaches are already harvested, the dewberries will be back every spring, and my summer greens have done well this year. If I get tomato blight on the fall crop, that would be a tragedy, but let's not think about that."

"I'm sure you won't," she said. "And at least no one's died on the farm, right?"

"At least not yet," I said, half-jokingly. "But now that you mention it, I think someone vandalized the Ulrich house."

"What do you mean?"

"They cut some of the cables Ed was using to brace the house. It almost fell down on Nick Schmidt's head today when he was in there working."

"That's terrible!" she said. "Who would do something like that?"

"I don't know," I said. "It makes me nervous to think someone was on my property messing with things and I didn't know about it. What if they decided to hurt my animals?"

"Chuck didn't bark or anything?"

"No," I said. "He used to bark every time a pecan dropped, but I think he's gotten so used to the cows and goats making noise that he's oblivious to anything short of a meteor strike. I sleep better because of it—usually—but it was kind of nice knowing he was on guard."

"Particularly with someone sneaking around and sabotaging your property," Quinn said as we got into line for a bratwurst, right behind Flora Kocurek and her boyfriend, Gus.

"Oh, Lucy! I heard you were there when they found Felix!" Flora gushed as she turned and spotted me.

"I was," I confirmed.

"Was he really in a beer barrel?"

"No," I said.

"I heard someone did him in with a pitchfork," Gus reported.

"Not that, either," I said. "There was an accident; something fell on him."

"Whatever it was must have weighed a ton," Flora said. "And I heard Teena Marburger went to the hospital with an epileptic fit."

"I don't think it was epilepsy. And I don't know if she went to the hospital," I said. Which reminded me, I needed to check on her. "She fainted, but she seemed to be coming to."

"I also heard she said something about a haunting!"

"Uh, not that I heard," I said. She'd said that cryptic stuff about something repeating, but that wasn't out of the ordinary for Teena, who was psychic. Or for someone recovering from a faint. What, I wondered briefly, did "It's repeating" mean, anyway?

"It's so sad, but also kind of exciting," Flora continued. "I mean, here we are with all these beers and pretzels and the oompah band and the decorations and all, feeling like we're living in Germany, and then there's a murder."

"Who said it was murder?"

"Well, somebody had to drop a heavy thing on him," she said. "Unless you think it was suicide?"

"How would you manage to drop something on your own head?" Gus asked.

"Good point. Murder, then," Flora said, playing with the blue ribbons in her hair. "His brother must just be so upset. But I hear they weren't getting along anyway."

Flora seemed rather hooked into the gossip circuit. I was impressed. "No?" I replied. "What did you hear?"

"I heard that Felix wanted to keep everything small, but Simon was like, 'Go big or go home.' And that he said he wasn't going to let Felix stand in the way of making Sweetwater Brewery a success."

That was kind of what I'd gathered from what the conversation I'd overheard, too. That Flora knew it too wasn't good news for Simon. "Where did you hear that?"

"Oh, everybody knows it," Flora said, waving a beringed hand.

"What else have you heard?"

"Well, I know about the whole barley fiasco. Adriana is fit to be tied. And then there's that talk about Felix's shady past."

My ears perked up. "What shady past?"

"Word is he was into some trouble before his brother invited him to go into business. If it weren't for Simon, Felix would be out on the street."

"What kind of trouble?"

Flora shrugged. "I don't know, but I got the impression he'd been doing something dodgy."

"I haven't heard anything about that," I said. Not that that was saying much. I hadn't heard anything about all the gossip she'd relayed until an hour earlier. And it seemed like whatever her information source was, it was valid. "Where are you getting all of this stuff, anyway?" she said.

"Oh, Gus and I have been hanging out at the Hitching Post lately," she said, referring to the bar on the town square. "The only things to do there are drink and talk, so there's plenty of both."

"I haven't been there in a while... maybe Tobias and I need to go get a drink there sometime."

"We go most nights," Flora said, then she added almost conspiratorially, "It's been so fun; after all those years cooped up at home, I finally have friends, it feels like."

"I'm so happy for you," I told her. And I meant it. "If you hear anything else, will you be sure to let me know?"

"Of course," she said. "Are you investigating?"

"No," I said. "I'm just... I'm worried that Rooster might put the wrong person in jail."

"So it was foul play," she breathed.

"I don't know if it was or not," I said, although something told me it was. "But he's already giving Simon a hard time about it. There's a chance he'll leap to a conclusion whether it's the right one or not."

"The easy way out," she said. "I heard he's trying to work less so he can be with his wife more."

Was work the problem? I wondered. Or hanging out with his buddies hunting or fishing? "Lacey sure wasn't happy with him for responding to a call today, that's for sure," I said.

"So he's more likely to go for a quick solution," Gus said. He'd been listening intently.

"Exactly," I said. "So if you hear anything..."

"We'll let you know," Flora promised.

TEENA, as it turned out, was fine; she had a small bump on her head, but other than that, she seemed unscathed. She'd declined a trip to the emergency room, instead promising to visit her primary care physician the next day. As the festival-goers poured out of the front gate, a few employees handed out coupons for free beer. I wasn't sure how good that would be for business, unfortunately. If the Gustafson brothers really were behind on their mortgage, giving away more free product wouldn't help. Unless Felix had had a life insurance policy, I thought...

I pushed the thought away. Until I heard otherwise, what had happened to Felix was an accident.

Except it wasn't.

Tobias looked grim when I saw him not far from the brewhouse.

"Any news?" I asked.

"It's looking like murder," he told me.

$\mathcal{M}$y stomach clenched. "Murder? Why?"

"Someone had to release that bag," he said. "It didn't fall by itself."

"Oh, no. That's horrible news."

"Rooster told Simon not to leave town."

I glanced around at all the festive bunting, the flowers, and the rows of food and beer stalls. "This Oktoberfest didn't exactly work out as planned, did it?"

"No," he said. As he spoke, I saw Max Pfeiffer, walking with a bratwurst in one hand and what looked like a Coke in the other. He was a short, thick man with a combover that barely covered his shiny scalp; in fact, as he took a bite of bratwurst, a stray breeze lifted it a few inches above his head. He didn't seem to notice.

"I still can't figure out what Max is doing here," I said. "I thought he swore never to set foot in the brewery."

"Checking out the competition?" Tobias asked.

"Or fouling that beer barrel and then taking out the head brewer?" I suggested.

"He does look rather pleased with himself," Tobias said.

"I hope Rooster looks into what's going on with him," I said.

"I don't think that's at the top of his list right now," Tobias said, tilting his head toward a large oak tree about twenty yards away. Rooster and Lacey stood beneath it. His arms were crossed over his chest, his eyes on the ground. Lacey was gesticulating; I couldn't hear what she was saying, but she didn't sound happy. Their kids were watching them wide-eyed, the funnel cakes in their hands forgotten.

"No, probably not," I said. Then my eyes strayed back to Max. He was talking with someone next to the elotes booth; it was the neatly dressed woman who'd been conferring with Simon earlier.

"Let's go get some corn," I suggested.

"I thought you wanted funnel cakes..." Tobias began, then he saw what I meant. "But roasted corn sounds great."

Together we headed to the elotes booth, which was being womanned by a server I recognized from Rosita's, the local Mexican restaurant.

"...after what's happened today, maybe we'd be willing to take a second look," the woman was saying as we drew close.

"That would be great," Max said. "I just did a major upgrade, and I'm about to hire..."

"What can I get you?" asked the woman behind the booth brightly. Max and the mystery woman glanced at us and moved further away.

"Um... one elote, please," I said, my mouth watering at the sight of the roasted corn. It wasn't exactly German— roasted corn was Mexican street food—but I didn't care.

"Coming right up," she said. "You want some crema on that?"

"Sure," I said, watching as she squirted some Mexican sour cream over the ear of corn, which had been coated in salt, chile powder, lime and butter, and handed it to me. Tobias had moved closer to Max and his conversational partner, pretending to be interested in an oak gall hanging from one of the outer branches of the tree. They drifted on, though, and mingled with the people still milling around the stalls, talking animatedly about the events of the day.

"Catch anything else?" I asked Tobias as I walked up to him, corn in hand.

"No," he said, "but it looks like Max may be profiting from what went on here today."

"That's definitely a motive," I said, sinking my teeth into the corn. "Oh. Oh, my."

"That good?" Tobias asked.

I nodded and handed him the corn, still chewing. He took a bite and moaned. We stood in culinary bliss for a few minutes, handing the corn back and forth and taking bites until both of our faces were coated in chile powder and crema. "Napkin," I muttered, and hurried back to the booth to grab a handful. We finished the corn and wiped off the worst of the damage—I'd gotten my T-shirt with a dollop of crema, and Tobias was sprinkled with chile powder—before we resumed our conversation.

"I think we should find out who she is," I said.

"I saw her business card," he said. "She handed it to him. I don't know her title, but she works for Brewlific Distributors."

I remembered the argument between Felix and Simon earlier that day. "That was who Simon was talking to, if I remember correctly. After what happened today, I'm guessing the deal with Sweetwater Brewery might be in jeopardy."

"Actually, it may be easier with Felix gone. I asked around and found out the brothers owned the business fifty-

fifty; they both had to sign on the dotted line to move forward with anything, and more and more, Felix was vetoing all of Simon's ideas. So if they can get past the bad press..."

"So Felix really was standing in the way of the business growing."

"Sounds like it. The good news for Simon—not that it's saying much—is that with Max Pfeiffer in the mix, at least Simon's not the only one with a motive for killing Felix."

"Speaking of other suspects, what was in the bag that fell on top of Felix?" I asked.

"Barley," Tobias told me.

"That's what I thought," I said. "Did you happen to see Adriana here today?"

"I did," Tobias confirmed. "She was sitting at a table under a tree with a mug of beer and a barbecue sandwich. Why?"

"She had a bone to pick with the Gustafson brothers. They contracted to buy her barley crop—it was the first time she tried growing it—but they rejected it. She's saying he might be bankrupted."

"How fitting to kill Felix with someone else's barley then," Tobias said.

"I don't know if that's what happened, of course, but it's worth thinking about. Plus, if she was so angry at the Gustafsons, why was she here at a promotional event?"

"The whole town was here," Tobias pointed out.

"Still."

"I see your point. But will Rooster think about it?"

"That's why we've got Deputy Shames," I said.

"Let's just hope she can talk sense into him." Tobias paused. "Although we don't know that Simon wasn't responsible."

"No," I said. "We don't. But I'd like to make sure the wrong person doesn't end up in jail."

"Again," Tobias said.

"Exactly."

WE SAW Teena as we were leaving; she was at the front gate again, her braided hair coming out of its plaits, her dirndl smudged with dirt, and a bit of mascara streaked under her big eyes. "Why are you still here?" I asked. "Shouldn't you go home and rest?"

"I had to help out," she said, attempting to tuck a loose tuft of hair back into its braid. "The paramedics said I was fine, so I figured I'd get back to work."

"I'm so relieved you're okay; when you went down, I was really worried."

"I think it was just... well, the shock of it. It's been a pretty awful day." She took a deep, shaky breath and swiped at her eyes. "I just don't know how things are going to go on without him."

I reached out and squeezed her hand. "I'm so sorry; you've worked so hard to make this event a success, and with what's happened, everything's gone sideways."

"I... I just can't believe Felix is gone!" she moaned. I held out my arms instinctively, and she moved toward me. I hugged her, stroking her hair as she sobbed into my shoulder. It was at least a minute before she let me go and stepped away. "I'm so sorry," she mumbled, embarrassed.

"No need to be sorry," I reassured her. "I'm here for you. We all are."

"We are," Tobias repeated.

"Not everyone is, I'm afraid," she said with a weak smile.

"What do you mean?" Tobias asked.

"It's just... you know," she shrugged. "Tensions at work and all. Normal stuff."

I waited for her to elaborate, but she didn't. "I meant to ask... you said something just as you fainted, but I didn't catch it. Do you remember what it was?"

Teena shook her head, and her eyes grew misty, as if she was seeing something in the distance. The hairs prickled on the back of my neck. Was this another one of what Teena called her magical foresight moments? "No," she said, finally. "But I had a flash of... of foreboding. Something about the past coming back again."

As she spoke, Tobias's phone rang. "I should take this; hang on a moment," he said, and excused himself to take the call.

"Are you sure you're doing okay?" I asked as Tobias stepped away.

"Not really," she said, and her eyes filled up with tears. "I just... he was just such a wonderful man," she said.

"I'm so sorry," I said. "I got the impression you and he might be... well, more than just friends."

"How did you know?" Her face flamed. "Promise you won't tell anyone," she whispered, glancing around furtively as if someone might be listening.

"I promise," I said. "Let's go over under that tree for a moment," I said, thinking she'd be more comfortable sharing away from the crowd. She nodded, then followed me. "Were you seeing him, then?" I asked once we were away from the main gate.

"We'd been dating for about two months," she said. "We had to keep it quiet, though. Felix said he shouldn't, but he just liked me so much... and that his brother would have a fit if he found out." She reached out and grabbed my arm. "Promise you won't tell anyone?"

"I'm not going to. Not unless I get asked by law enforcement," I amended.

Her eyes widened. "Why would they ask you that?"

I shrugged. "If it turns out to be foul play, they're going to be asking all kinds of questions," I said gently. "You might have to tell them the truth."

"My dad will kill me," she said.

"I'm sure you'll be fine," I reassured her. "He's just looking after you. I know you're legally an adult, but you're still his little girl."

"He's just so... overprotective," she said. "I'm not a kid anymore."

"I know, but parents have a hard time letting go," I told her. "I know it's annoying, but he's just trying to take care of you." Personally, I thought she was too young to be dating Felix, too. Plus, she was still living at home, which made it harder to change the parent-child relationship to one of two adults. Maybe at some less-charged time, I might be able to bring that up, but now was not the time.

"Did anyone else know you and Felix were seeing each other?"

She bit her lip, but didn't say anything.

"Teena?"

"Well," she said slowly, "one person found out today."

"What do you mean?"

"I was back in the warehouse with Felix; I was helping him pick out the barrel he wanted brought to the tasting. We were about to go our separate ways, and he gave me a kiss. When I turned to go, I saw Nick standing in the doorway."

"So Nick saw the kiss," I said.

"I don't know for sure," she said, "but probably. He looked pretty torqued. He wouldn't say anything to me; he just turned and stalked away."

"What was he doing in the warehouse?" I asked.

"That's a good question," she said. "He doesn't work here. Maybe he followed me? Or was looking for me?"

"Why would he do that?" I asked, as if I didn't know that Nick was head-over-heels for young Teena.

She shrugged. "He asked me out a few times. I think he likes me."

I thought about the fouled barrel of beer. "While you were there, did you mark the beer you planned to open at the tasting?"

She nodded. "I wrote FOR TASTING on a piece of paper and taped it to the barrel."

"When did this happen?"

"Right after the gates opened," she said. "Probably around ten this morning."

"Is the warehouse usually locked?" I asked.

"Usually, but not today, I don't think," she said. "We've been in and out all the time, restocking."

"So anyone could have figured out which barrel was being used for the tasting and done something to it."

She blinked. "I guess you're right; I didn't think about that. You think that's what happened?"

"I have no idea what happened," I said, "but it sure means that just about anyone could have done it."

"Why would someone do something like that?"

I shrugged. "A bone to pick with the brewery? Or with Felix?"

"But he was so nice!" Teena protested, with the innocence of youth. "Why would anyone want to do something bad to him?"

"People do bad things sometimes," I told her. "We've both seen it."

"I know," she said. And then she blinked. "Oh."

"What?"

"I remember the word now. It was revenge."

"Revenge?" I asked.

She shrugged. "It must have something to do with what happened today. The problem is, I have no idea what it is."

And neither did I.

Tobias walked back over to us as we pondered the word. "I've got to run out to a case," he told me. "Want to come with me?"

"What is it?" I asked.

"The Froehlichs' cattle started having trouble. It all started at once; he wants me to take a look."

I turned to Teena. "Are you going to be okay?"

She nodded and lifted her chin. "I'll be fine."

"It'll take a while, likely," I told her. "I'm around, though, if you need to talk."

She gave me a small, forlorn smile. "Thanks, Lucy."

"WHAT WAS UP WITH THAT?" Tobias asked as we headed out to the field where we'd parked our trucks.

"Just between you and me," I told him, "Teena was dating Felix."

"Wasn't he kind of old for her?" he asked.

"That's what I thought, too, but she seems drawn to older guys. Which isn't good news for Nick."

"I saw him watching her. He looks smitten."

"He is. And here's some news: apparently he saw her kissing Felix in the warehouse earlier today. Teena said he looked angry and wouldn't talk to her. Plus, she marked the barrel for the tasting ahead of time, so anyone could have gone in, found it, and fouled it."

"Presuming they were able to open it," Tobias pointed out. "I'm not sure exactly how that works."

"We'll have to find out," I said.

"This does give us another person with a motive for Felix's death, though, doesn't it?"

"Do you really think Nick would kill Felix because he kissed Teena? He's such a nice kid!" I protested.

"I don't know," Tobias said as we reached his truck. He unlocked my door and opened it for me, then went around to his side. He waited until he'd closed the driver's side door to answer. "Young men and women are pretty passionate creatures. I don't like to think he could have done something like that, but maybe the opportunity presented itself and he took it..."

"Maybe," I said, doubtfully. "But what happened doesn't exactly seem like a crime of passion. Whoever dropped that bag on Felix had to think about it. Had to have it in position and have some reason to be in the brewery, in exactly the right place, at exactly the right time."

Tobias turned the key in the ignition. "And whoever dropped the bag had to have enough knowledge of how the machinery worked to move it into place. Nick does work in construction," he pointed out.

"Yes, but that's different from working in a brewery."

"Still. He has at least some mechanical knowledge. How hard would it be to figure out?"

"I can't imagine that Nick would do something like that."

Tobias put the truck in reverse and began backing out of the space. "Two minutes ago you were telling me you couldn't imagine Simon killing Felix. Now you're coming up with lots of reasons why he was the perfect candidate."

"How I feel about it emotionally is one thing," I said. "I would hate for someone so young to screw up the rest of his life because he felt rejected."

"Not to mention screwing up the rest of Felix's life," Tobias pointed out.

"True," I said, and sighed. "Not quite the Oktoberfest opener I was hoping for."

"No," he said. "Let's just hope the rest of the week doesn't follow suit."

7

_T_obias and I drove up the bumpy driveway to the farm just as dusk was falling. He kept me company while I did my chores, checking over everyone as I milked the cows and goats.

"They look okay?" I asked, somewhat fretfully. We'd stopped by the Froehlichs' to check on their cattle on the way back to Dewberry Farm; several of them were a little bit lame. Tobias wasn't sure what was wrong, but he had taken blood samples to send to a lab, and I was worried that whatever it was might be catching.

"They do," he said. "None of the symptoms the Froehlichs' stock have."

"Thank heavens," I said, relieved. After the failure of all of my cucurbit plants and the news of the rash of sick livestock in the area, I was feeling particularly anxious.

"So far, so good," he said, stroking Blossom's ear as Gidget nibbled at his jeans. "Hey," he said. "Stop that!"

"She took the tea bag right out of my mug yesterday morning," I said as I finished milking Hot Lips. The goat licked the last bit of feed out of the feeder I'd put up for her at the end of the milking stall and then bolted out to grab hold of Tobias's other jeans leg. "They're certainly not low-energy," Tobias said, chuckling as he pried his jeans away from the two goats.

"Either that or you're just delicious," I said, grinning. He gave Hot Lips a quick check, and then we walked out of the barn toward the gate, trailing goats and cows.

"And there's what used to be my pumpkin crop," I said, pointing out the rows of ravaged plants as we squeezed through the gate and latched it behind us. With everything that had happened today, I'd forgotten to tell him.

"Oh, Lucy... I'm so sorry. They were looking so good!"

"I know," I said. "It's melon worm, apparently... due to the weather. I have to destroy all the plant matter and spray bT to keep the infestation down going forward. I hope it's not a permanent thing; cucumbers, summer squash and melons are in the same family. I always get a great cucumber crop, and make lots of pickles."

"I'm sure you'll get it under control," he said, then surveyed the wasteland that had been my pumpkin patch. "Next season, anyway."

I sighed.

"Ever think about raising pigs?" he asked, changing the subject.

"No," I said. "I love bacon, but I just can't bring myself to raise animals to slaughter. I'd have a farm full of happy pigs, go completely bankrupt, and never eat breakfast sausage again."

He laughed. "I totally understand. Why do you think I became a vet? I'm a softie, too." The breeze ruffled the grass as we walked over to the chicken coop, where the hens were already starting to roost. My new Brahma rooster, Russell Crow, was still on the small side, but before long he would be two feet tall and very capable of keeping the ladies safe. He was now proudly strutting among a few of the hens, including my favorites, Niblet and Bready, both of whom had a habit of hunkering down to be picked up. Until this year, I hadn't had a rooster, but Tobias had convinced me it might be a good idea, so I'd decided to give it a shot.

I'd worked with Russell since he was a chick (he'd just hatched that last spring). He had feathered out and was starting to look like a rooster, and had recently begun practicing his crow, but he was still young. Although he would eventually be big enough, and feisty enough, to scare off small predators, he'd been kind and gentle with the girls and with us so far; I hoped it lasted.

He came over to greet us, along with Bready, who doing her hunkering maneuver. As Tobias cooed to Russell, I reached down and lifted her gently, admiring her red-gold feathers, which were beautiful in the waning sun. I gave her a few pets as Tobias and Russell Crow looked on, then released her to join the rooster and the rest of the flock. As dedicated as I was to eating meat that came from traditionally farm-raised animals, I hadn't yet made enough of a transition from city girl to country girl to start dispatching my beloved livestock.

Once Russell and the girls were settled for the night, we went into the farmhouse, where I began processing the milk as we talked about all the goings-on at Oktoberfest.

"I was telling Quinn that I think the Gustafsons might have been in trouble at the brewery," I told him as I poured the milk into a big pot and turned on the stove.

"What do you mean?"

"I saw a notice from the mortgage company when we walked over to the farmhouse," I said. "It's past due."

"If they're behind, it would explain why Simon was so

interested in expanding the business," Tobias said, coming to the same conclusion I had earlier.

"By the way, I found out a little bit more about the woman was he was talking to," he added.

"Oh?"

"Yeah. I knew she was with Brewlific, so I looked the company up; evidently they're a very big co-op distributor."

"And?"

"If you sign with them, your beers are made in breweries all over the country," he said.

"No wonder Felix didn't like that."

"But I can see why Simon did... it massively expands your reach."

"And your profits," I said, giving the milk a stir and reaching into the fridge to grab each of us a Bluff lager. "They put a lot of money into that place; if it meant more money coming in, I can see why Simon would want to sign up."

Tobias leaned back in his chair, considering me from blue eyes that were the color of cornflowers and made my heart accelerate a few beats. "So do you think he got Felix out of the way so that he could?" he asked.

"I'm not sure about that yet," I replied as I sat down at the table next to him. "It seems like the obvious choice, but did you see the look on his face when he saw his brother? He looked shaken to the core."

"Good actor?" Tobias suggested, reaching out to play with my hair and brushing my neck with his fingers.

"Maybe," I said, leaning into his touch. "But there are a lot of other players involved who might have had it in for the brothers. And Simon would never have tampered with the brewery's beer right as they were about to do a reveal. Bad for business."

"True," Tobias said. "Max Pfeiffer was about to sue over the use of the Bluff name," he said, turning the beer bottle around in his hand and looking at the label.

"I was surprised to see him there today, honestly. And then there's the Adriana Janacek thing."

"The failed barley crop," Tobias said. "If it bankrupted her, I can see why she'd be angry and upset. That farm's been in the family for generations."

"Small business is risky, isn't it?" I asked, feeling a twinge of nervousness. "Thank goodness I'm diversifying. Although I've had a few setbacks myself."

"What do you mean?"

"Well, first there's the melon worm problem. Then there's the Ulrich house, which almost fell down on Nick today."

"You mentioned that," he said. "And Ed thinks someone sabotaged it?"

"He does," I said. "Which makes me worry. If it had fallen down..." I shivered.

"I can imagine," he said. "Anything else gone wrong lately? Any signs of someone tampering with things?"

"No, not that I've noticed," I told him. "But I'm going to be a lot more mindful." I got up to check on the milk. "I'm going to try experimenting a bit, I think," I said as I gave the pot a stir.

"What are you thinking?" he asked.

"I've always done fresh goat cheese, but never experimented with aged goat cheese." I glanced at him. "Diversification, after all."

"Right," he said, grinning. "Well, if you need a test subject, I'm always willing to take one for the team."

"You're too kind," I said. As I spoke, there was a crowing sound from outside. "Is that Russell?"

"Sounds like it," Tobias said, springing to his feet as the rooster crowed again. "And sounds like there might be trouble."

We hurried to the kitchen door; as I opened it, I could hear the chickens clucking loudly, and Russell let out another, anxious-sounding crow. Tobias followed me to the coop. As we got there, a raccoon slunk out a hole in the roof of the coop, then scampered across the roof ridge and leapt into a nearby oak tree.

"Russell's doing his job already," Tobias said approvingly. "But when did that hole in your coop roof get there?"

"It's the first I've seen of it," I told him. Near the roofline, the corner of the corrugated metal roof had been pried up.

"Looks like the raccoon may have pulled it up," Tobias said. "Got a ladder?"

"In the barn," I said. "I'll fetch it, along with some nails and a hammer."

With Tobias spotting me, I pushed the metal back down and nailed it back in place—he'd offered to do it for me, but I'd insisted on taking care of it myself—and then, when the flock was safe, we returned the ladder to the barn and headed back to the house.

As I opened the door to the kitchen, the sound of a smoke detector blared, and the smell of burnt milk billowed out.

I'd forgotten about the milk on the stove.

I ran over to turn off the burner, but I was far too late; the milk had spilled all over the stove and down onto the floor, where Chuck was lapping at it. I said a few choice words and inspected the stovetop, which was covered in cooked-on milk.

"Is it ruined?" Tobias asked as he grabbed a roll of paper towels and tackled the part of the floor Chuck hadn't already cleaned up. He'd taken care of the smoke detector while I turned off the stove.

"The stove, or the milk?"

He tore off several sheets of paper towel and wiped the front of the oven. "Both."

I sighed. "The stove will survive, although it's going to be hard to get the milk out of all those crevices, but I'm pretty sure the milk itself is toast. I'm guessing it burned to the bottom of the pot, and now the whole thing tastes off."

"If you had pigs, they'd love it," Tobias said.

"No pigs," I said. We spent the next twenty minutes cleaning up. By the time we'd tossed the last of the paper towels into the compost bin, the milk was cool enough to taste.

"What do you think?" I asked.

"You know what? It tastes a little like flan."

I took a taste. "You're right," I said. "It's a little bit caramelized, isn't it?"

"Maybe you should sell flan at the Oktoberfest market," he suggested.

"But it's goat's milk."

"Cajeta is made with goat's milk."

"What's that?" I asked.

"Mexican caramel sauce," he said. "Let's try a batch. I know you have eggs, right?"

"I do," I said. "I just need a flan recipe."

"Give me thirty seconds," he said, pulling out his phone. A moment later, he turned the phone to show me. "Goat milk crème caramel," he said. "A flan by any other name..."

I laughed. "What do we need? Eggs, milk, vanilla..."

"And sugar," he said, turning the phone back around and reading the ingredients list. "That's it. Do you have ramekins you can use?"

"I actually bought a bunch of foil ones just last week," I said. "If they work, we can sell them in the ramekins."

"Let's do a practice run. If it works, we'll make more."

"You're brilliant," I said.

"If only my calculus professor agreed with you," he said.

I grinned. "Not your favorite class?"

"I almost quit being pre-vet after the mid-term exam," he said. "I still have nightmares."

"Poor you," I said. "Glad you were persistent, though. And I know Chuck is, too."

As Tobias gathered sugar and vanilla from the pantry, I reviewed the recipe on Tobias's phone, then retrieved the metal ramekins from the bedroom I used for crafting and pulled a roasting pan from the drawer under the oven. "I have to make caramel, don't I?"

"Yup," Tobias agreed.

I sighed. I didn't usually have good luck with caramel. "If you'll do the rest of the recipe, I'll attempt caramel."

"Sounds like a division of labor that works for me." I greased the ramekins, then measured out the sugar and poured it into a small saucepan. "I'm not supposed to stir it, apparently," I said, looking at the recipe. "Maybe that's what I've been doing wrong."

"We'll find out," Tobias said as he cracked an egg into a bowl.

IT TOOK FOUR TRIES, but I finally managed to get a batch of caramel that didn't granulate or burn in the saucepan. "Here goes nothing," I said as I slid the roasting pan loaded with ramekins into the oven, then used the kettle to add hot water to the pan, making a hot water bath for the custards. I set the timer as Tobias rinsed the bowl out. Then we retreated to the couch in the living room, Chuck happily snuggled up between us.

"Well," he said. "We've taken care of your chores, fixed the roof, and made a trial batch of flan. I think we've been very productive."

"And don't forget looked after the Froehlichs' cattle," I said. "What do you think's going on there, anyway?"

"I don't know yet," he said, "but I've had a few calls this week. I'll have to do a little more research, see if they're isolated incidents or if there's a common thread."

"Mine are okay, though, right?"

"They sure look okay to me," he said, putting an arm around me. "You take good care of your animals. With the possible exception of Chuck's diet, that is."

I rolled my eyes. "I really think he's just big-boned."

"Uh huh," he said. "I saw you slip him that leftover bratwurst when we got home."

"I don't know what you're talking about," I said, blushing. As I spoke, there was a scratching sound from the fireplace. Chuck's ears perked up, and he growled. "What's that?" I asked.

"Hopefully not another raccoon," he said.

"Man, I hope not, either," I said, getting up and walking over to the fireplace. There was another scratching sound, and Chuck leapt off the couch and ran to the fireplace, barking.

"Easy, boy," Tobias said.

"Could be a bird?" I suggested.

"Could be," he said. As he spoke, though, another sound came from the chimney. And it was entirely unbirdlike.

8

"*I*s that what I think it was?" I asked Tobias.

He squatted down and stuck his head into the chimney. "Do you have a flashlight?"

"I'll grab one from the kitchen," I said, and hurried to retrieve one as Tobias peered up into the dark chimney and Chuck stood on the hearth, barking.

I jogged back into the living room and handed Tobias the flashlight. "Is the flue open?" he asked.

"Probably not," I said. "It hasn't been cold enough for a fire since February."

He reached up in and gently pulled on the flue handle. The scratchy meowing intensified. A moment later, a little black-and-gray ball tumbled down; Tobias caught it just in time.

"Is it okay?" I asked, anxious. Chuck had stopped barking, and was now sniffing curiously at the tuft of fur Tobias was holding.

Tobias cradled the little body in his hands and probed it gently. "Nothing obviously broken," he said in a soft voice, "but I'm guessing she's a little dehydrated. It's hard to tell, but I think this is a girl. I wonder if she's got any siblings up there?"

"I'll look," I said, retrieving the flashlight from the hearth where he'd set it. As Tobias gently examined the little gray kitten, I craned my neck and looked up the chimney. "Nobody else that I can see," I announced.

"She must have come from somewhere," Tobias said. "Any of your neighbors have kittens?"

"Not that I know of. I'll ask around, though. How old is she?"

"Four or five weeks, I'd guess," he said.

"How did she get up there?" I asked.

"I have no idea," he said. "I'm surprised she's so far from her mother, though."

"I've seen a cat around on and off over the last few months," I said. "I think I told you about her; she's a gray tabby, and I think she's feral."

"I remember," he said, stroking the kitten's dirty head. It gave a tiny little meow and then began to purr, a raspy, rumbling sound that vibrated her whole body. "You borrowed the Have-A-Heart trap to see if you could catch her to get her spayed."

"I did," I said, stroking the kitten's soft head. "But all I got was a raccoon."

"Who evidently is still hanging around the place, if the chicken coop incident is any indication," he said. "Have you seen the cat recently?"

I shook my head. "Last time was a few weeks ago, I think," I said.

"I'm guessing she holed up somewhere safe and had kittens," Tobias said. "Maybe we should go look for them; but first, let's get this one some food and then get her cleaned up."

"How do we do that?" I asked.

"Fortunately, I'm an experienced kitten washer," he said with a grin. "Plus, if you'll hold her, I've got some kitten chow and milk in the truck."

"What?"

"Spring and summer is kitten season," he said. "I always keep some in my kit, just in case."

"You're amazing," I said. A few minutes later, Tobias fed the tiny cat with a syringe. I was relieved to see her lapping it up with her little pink tongue; aside from the soot all over her bedraggled coat, she seemed to be doing fairly well.

The timer beeped on the oven as we worked; I took out the flans, which had browned to a beautiful creamy gold and didn't look at all as if they'd curdled or separated, and arranged them on a rack to cool. Once the oven was turned off, together, using soft cloths and lukewarm water, we gently cleaned the kitten in the kitchen sink as she mewed in protest. She was covered in soot, making the water run almost black, and I found myself wondering if she would change colors as we cleaned her.

Most of her stayed gray, but as we cleaned her, a white streak on her nose and the left side of her face and a white patch on her stomach and chest appeared, along with four cute white socks. Her whiskers, once clean, were snow white, a striking contrast to her charcoal-colored fur, and her eyes were a striking green. "She looks like a gray tuxedo cat," Tobias said. The kitten let out a scratchy meow.

"She's beautiful," I said. "What should we call her?"

Tobias cocked an eyebrow at me. "Are we keeping her?"

I shrugged. "I could use a mouser," I said.

"She is pretty cute." He touched the white streak on her nose, and she let out another one of those rumbly purrs. "She seems to be in pretty good shape, thankfully; she must not have been in there too long. Let's get her settled some-place warm and see if we can find any others," he suggested.

I tucked the kitten into a box with a fluffy towel and tucked the box away in my bedroom before closing the door so that Chuck, who was extremely curious, wouldn't bother her.

"We should probably take Chuck with us," Tobias suggested, "but on a leash. He might help us find any others, but if he does, I'd rather be able to keep them apart."

"Makes sense," I said. Together, we headed out in to the dark, Chuck not quite sure what to do with a leash on him —we'd kind of abandoned it since moving to Buttercup from Houston.

"Can you find more kittens?" I asked Chuck, as if he could understand English.

He seemed to get the idea. Nose to the ground, my scruffy apricot poodle sniffed around the base of the house until he got to the bottom of the oak tree whose branches scraped the roof near the chimney. I'd been meaning to trim it back, but had never quite gotten there.

"Anyone up there?" I asked.

"Hard to see through the leaves," Tobias responded, shining his flashlight up into the branches. "I don't hear anything, though."

"And Chuck's not barking."

"True, but Chuck didn't start barking at the kitten in the chimney until it started meowing," Tobias pointed out. I couldn't argue with him. Chuck had many redeeming quali-ties, but his skill as a hunter was not one of them.

We stood at the base of the tree for some time, but Chuck seemed mainly interested in the patch of licorice-scented fennel I'd planted under the living room window; if there were any felines in the tree, he paid them no notice. I certainly didn't see or hear anything. After a few minutes we walked around the tool shed and the little building that my grandmother used to use to smoke bacon in; these days, I used it to dry onions and potatoes. Chuck got a little more interested as we got closer, his floppy ears pricking up a few millimeters and his nose almost glued to the ground. I opened the door just in time to see something slip out a hole in the back. Chuck barked and growled menacingly, but stuck close to me.

"That looked like it might have been mama," I said to Tobias.

"Maybe she had her kittens in here, then," he said. He shone the flashlight around. In the corner, there was a little round of hay that looked as if it had been slept in by something the size of a cat. "This is probably it," he said.

"No more kittens, though."

"No. At least not in here," he said. "I wonder if the raccoon got to them."

"That's a horrible thought!"

"It happens sometimes," he said grimly. He shone the flashlight all around the shed, but there was no sign of any more kittens. We walked around outside; as he shone his flashlight down toward the pasture, we got a flash of eyeshine.

"There she is," he said. "Time to get out the Have A Heart trap again, my dear. We need to get that girl spayed."

"You're right," I said. "I wish we could find the other kittens."

"I think ours may be the only one. Maybe she managed to escape when the raccoon got in."

"How did she get all the way up that tree?"

"Maybe her mom carried her?" Tobias suggested. "She

might have put her in the chimney to keep her safe? We'll probably never know."

"Let's do one more sweep, just in case."

We walked around the house one more time, but found nothing, and Chuck didn't show any signs of scenting anything interesting. We headed back inside. As Tobias snuggled Chuck on the couch, I checked on the kitten in the bedroom. She had curled up into a little gray and white ball and was fast asleep. My eyes drifted to the dark window; her mom was out there somewhere, maybe looking for her lost kittens.

I wished I could find some way to let her know we were taking care of her little girl.

9

I got to the Blue Onion just before three the next day; I spent the morning milking, clearing out more dead plants, taking care of the kitten, and making mozzarella cheese. I'd gotten the hang of making mozzarella over the summer—it was fairly easy, involving fresh milk, rennet, citric acid, and a little salt. It was a bit of a process, as the milk had to be heated to precise temperatures twice, but it was fun squeezing the whey out of the curds (which always made me think of Miss Muffett), and even more fun stretching the cheese at the end, as if it were a giant wad of taffy.

Not as fun as eating it though; as usual, I treated myself to a mozzarella, basil, tomato and olive oil lunch, only sharing a little bit with Chuck, before tackling a less-pleasant task that generally involved airing out the kitchen for an hour or two: soap.

It was two before I left the kitchen with a new batch of soap (thankfully the cure time wasn't too long for the recipe I was using) and headed outside gathered more bouquets for Oktoberfest, almost picking my cutting garden clean. I surveyed my offerings before heading to the Blue Onion; I still had a few flans to sell, and plenty of beeswax candles, but I wished I had something else to fill out my stall.

Now, as I unloaded the cooler onto one of the butcher block counters of the Blue Onion, Quinn eyed the fresh cheese hungrily. The lunch hour was over, and Quinn had turned to baking for the Oktoberfest market. The cheerful kitchen was redolent with ginger and spices; my mouth watered at the scent of the gingerbread hearts she had just pulled out of the oven.

Quinn, evidently, was peckish as well. "Did you just make that this morning?" she asked.

"I did," I said.

"Can I try some?"

"Only if I can have some lebkuchen," I said, unwrapping one of the logs and slicing off the creamy end.

"It's a deal," she said, and popped the white disk into her mouth. "This is divine," she groaned. "Wow. Are you sure you didn't go to some special cheese-making school without telling me?"

I laughed. "It's really not that hard."

She grabbed the knife and cut herself another slice. "I may have to make mozzarella a regular feature. And those tomatoes look so good... and the basil." She groaned. "I'd better watch out or I'm not going to be able to tie my karate belt."

"How's that going, anyway?"

"I'm up for my black belt test in December," she said. I eyed my red-haired friend proudly; with her strong arms, straight back, and sunny smile, you'd never guess at her past, but Quinn's ex, Jed Stadtler, had abused her for years.

When she was finally able to extricate herself from the relationship, Quinn had taken up karate in case he came around again. Unfortunately, her knowledge had come in handy a time or two. Even though Jed was currently behind bars, my friend still had a tendency to be jumpy, and I knew the scars he'd left weren't only physical.

"How's training going?" I asked.

"Not well," she said with a grimace. "The holidays are coming, which is the busy time of year, and I've spent so much time baking I haven't made it to the dojo as often as I'd like."

"I'm sure you'll be fine," I said. "If I can help you out by picking up extra hours, I'm happy to... things slow down a little in late fall and winter, since I don't milk as often."

"That would be great," she said, looking up at me. A few ringlets had escaped the bandana she usually wore to keep her hair out of her eyes, and despite her smile, she looked tired. "I'm having a hard time keeping up with the training, and I'm worried I'm not going to pass."

"You'll pass with flying colors," I said with confidence. "And like I said, any help I can offer is yours."

"Thanks," she said, her smile growing bigger. "How are you with piping icing?"

"Umm..."

She laughed. "How about you mix up another batch of filling for the Bienenstich, then, and I'll take care of decorating?"

"That sounds like a better division of labor," I said, eyeing the beautifully decorated cookies she'd already finished making. "What goes into Bee... Beena... whatever you call that cake, anyway?"

"Bienenstich; Bee-nen-stitch, or bee sting cake in English. Honey, of course—hence the name. I'm using honey from Serafine's hives. Honeyed Moon started selling some honey in addition to the mead."

"I can supply you honey next year," I said. "If all goes well, my hives should be producing well."

"Here's hoping." She walked over to a golden sheet of pastry studded with glistening almonds; it looked delicious.

"So what's in it other than honey?" I asked.

"It's a yeast-based cake," she told me. "You let it rise, cover it with the honey-almond mixture, and bake it. Then you cut it in half to make two layers and fill it with a vanilla custard cream."

"Oh, wow," I said. "That explains why it smells so good in here."

"If you think that's good, wait until we do the lebkuchen and dip it in chocolate," she said.

"Chocolate dipping I'm good at," I said.

"If you'll whip up the custard cream, I'll take care of the gingerbread hearts and filling the Bienenstich and let you get started on the lebkuchen."

"Sounds like a plan," I said.

We spent the next two hours working companionably in the Blue Onion's delicious-smelling kitchen. I made a new batch of lebkuchen dough, first beating together sugar, honey, butter and orange zest and then combining the dry ingredients, including cocoa, flour, almond meal and spices, in second bowl. As I added eggs to the wet ingredients, I told Quinn about our adventures with the kitten.

"Are you going to keep her?" she asked.

"We'll see," I said. "I just hope we can figure out how to catch the mother and get her spayed."

"I hope you can too," she said as she put the finishing touches on another cookie. "How's it going over there?"

"I'm just about to put the dough in the fridge. Is there some from earlier I can use while this chills?"

"It's on the top shelf, labeled," she told me. "The scoop

for measuring batter is over there." She pointed to what looked like a small ice cream scoop hanging from a peg board over the counter.

"Got it," I said.

"You just wet your hands a little, roll the dough into a ball, and then press it down a little onto the parchment," she advised me. "Cookie sheets are on that rack over there, and there's a big roll of parchment paper in the pantry."

"Thanks," I said as she put down her white icing piper and retrieved a blue one. I put parchment on three baking sheets and began scooping out dough and rolling it between my hands, thankful I had this job. Quinn's gingerbread hearts were works of art, with lace-like piping and perfectly formed Edelweiss flowers and blue frosting ribbons. Mine, I knew, would have looked like something off of "Nailed It."

"So, are you keeping the kitten?"

"I don't know," I said, and she gave me a look. "All right. I'm 90 percent sure I am."

"Only 90? You've been saying you want a cat, and if Chuck is getting along with her..."

"I know," I said. "I've just got so much already, with the goats and the cows and Chuck and all the vegetables and the little orchard..."

"Speaking of vegetables, have you managed to get all those pumpkins cleared out yet?"

"No," I confessed as I rolled another ball of dough and pressed it onto the parchment, resisting the temptation to pop it into my mouth instead. "It's on the list. Maybe after Oktoberfest is over."

"That sounds like a plan," she said, then shot me a sidelong glance. "Plus, with all the hours you're spending investigating what happened to Felix Gustafson, I don't imagine you have a lot of spare time."

"Who told you that?"

"I heard you were asking about Adriana and the barley crop," she said, finishing another cookie with a flourish, "and I saw Mandy from the *Buttercup Zephyr* talking with you at the market last night. Find out anything good?"

"Maybe." I scooped up another ball of dough and rolled it between my palms. "I'm hearing rumors that Felix had some shady things in his past, and that part of the reason Simon started the brewery was to help him out."

"Shady things like what?" she asked.

"He was accused of embezzling at a brewery he worked at, apparently. It's not clear if he was really responsible or not, but it would be hard to get a job if that was the word on the street."

"Have you googled him?" Quinn asked as I pressed another ball onto the parchment-covered baking pan.

"Let me get these in the oven and I will," I told her. I hurried through the rest of the dough, popped the pans into the oven and then sat down at the laptop Quinn kept at the end of the counter. "Mind if I use this?"

"Go ahead," she said.

As she started icing another cookie, I brought up Google and typed in Felix Gustafson. An article came up immediately, about a brewery in Houston, called Swamp Thang Brewery, going under. The owner was listed as Bethany Jackson, and Felix was the head brewer, but there was nothing about embezzlement or any financial irregularities.

"There's an article about the brewery," I told Quinn, "which said nothing about embezzlement.." I googled Swamp Thang Brewery next. A slick profile from the Houston Chronicle came up, by a reporter whose name I recognized: it was one of my old friends from my time at the paper. The profile, which was dated five years earlier, featured a picture of Felix, his beard as thick and tangled as I remembered, sitting on a beer barrel next to a red-haired woman in a pair of faded jeans and a loose white blouse whose open neck highlighted a cluster of beer-related necklaces; I couldn't make out all of them, but I easily identified a barrel, a small bottle opener, and a beautiful, iridescent green bottle. The two faces were glowing with excitement and hope.

"Here's a profile on their new business," I said, and began reading the article. "Apparently they met when they were both working at the Golden Oaks Brewery in Houston," I reported to Quinn as I read. "They didn't like the way the place was run, so they found an investor and decided to strike out on their own."

"Who was the investor?" Quinn asked.

I scanned the article. "A venture capital firm called Liquid Assets, according to this."

"Clever name," she said. "Doesn't sound like it worked out."

"I guess you win some, you lose some." I switched over to Facebook and typed in Felix's name. "He wasn't super active on social media, it looks like."

"I'm surprised he was on at all," she said. "What are you looking for, anyway?"

"Connections," I said. "I don't know." He had a whopping six friends, one of whom was his brother. I clicked on Simon's name, and wasn't surprised to be directed to a page with a picture of Simon, beer in hand, smiling broadly in front of the Sweetwater Brewery sign. He had over a thousand friends. I scanned them, looking for anything that stuck out at me.

"I wish I knew the name of that woman he was talking to at the Oktoberfest event," I said.

"I do," Quinn said. "She got lunch in here that day; I took her credit card. It was Beth something. Kind of an ordinary name."

I typed BETH in the friends list. Two "Beths" popped up: one was Bethany Jackson, whose name I recognized from the article with Felix. The other was Beth Collins. I clicked on her profile.

"That's the one," I said when her profile picture came up.

Quinn abandoned her cookie decorating to come and peer over my shoulder. "Who is she?"

"She's friends with Simon, but not Felix."

"Who does she work for?"

"A company called Brewlific," I said. "She's a sales manager for the southwest region, apparently; she was at Sweetwater talking to Simon the day of the festival."

"What does Brewlific do?"

"It's some kind of consortium of craft brewers, it looks like." I opened a new window and googled "Beth Collins Brewlific." Her name came up, along with the same photo that was on her Facebook page.

"She looks a little like a 1980s corporate movie woman," Quinn said. "Not exactly the brewery image."

I stared at the image; she was a 30-something woman with dark brown hair cut in a sleep bob, a conservative black jacket, and a white silk shell; the only nod to the brewing industry was a gold necklace with an iridescent green bottle on it.

"That looks familiar," I said. I clicked back to the article spotlighting Swamp Thang brewery, and put the two side by side.

"They're wearing the same necklace," Quinn remarked as I magnified the picture.

"Look at the eyes," I said.

Quinn blinked. "Holy smokes. Is that the same person?"

"I think so," I said.

"Why did she change her name?"

I flipped back to Beth Collins's Facebook profile. Her relationship status was married. "I'm guessing Jackson was her maiden name," I said. "Maybe she shortened the Bethany to Beth when she reinvented herself as a corporate type."

"And that's how she knew about Sweetwater Brewery," Quinn said. "She and Felix ran Swamp Thang back in Houston."

"If they ended on bad terms, I can see why Felix wasn't a fan of joining forces with them."

"But if money was tight and the opportunity came up, it would be hard to turn down, I imagine." She shook her head. "No wonder they say not to mix business and family."

"Particularly when exes are involved," I said. I looked up the Bethany Jackson profile; no one had posted a new picture on it in four years, and everything else must have been set to private, as the only thing visible was her profile image. "I guess she just started a new profile and never got around to taking the old one down," I theorized.

"I wish I knew what happened between the two of them," Quinn said.

I glanced at her. "Are you thinking maybe it was a crime of passion?"

Quinn shrugged. "I don't know."

"It's worth considering," I said. "If he was part of the reason Swamp Thang didn't make it, I'd be pretty angry about it."

"And then he's trying to scuttle a new deal for her by refusing to let Sweetwater Brewery sign on..."

"I wish I could talk to her and find out what happened with the brewery in Houston."

"I think she's still in town," Quinn said. "She's staying at the hotel on the square; I overheard Simon talking about it to someone the other day."

"Are you suggesting I go and talk to her? On what pretext?"

"You could just tell her you're wondering if she can help you figure out what's going on?" she suggested.

"I don't know," I said. "I'll think about it." I closed up the computer. "But in the meantime, I'm going to finish up these cookies; I've got to get home and get ready for the market."

"I had one of your flans," she said. "It was delicious. Oh—and don't let me forget to pay you for the cheese and the veggies. And the time."

"We'll figure it out later," I told her. "I've got to run home and take care of the kitten; do you have the rest of this?"

"I'll glaze them drop a few off for you to sell at your booth," she said. "And once this is all over, if you still need help with those plants, let me know."

"I will," I said. "See you in a bit?"

"I can taste the bratwurst already," she said with a smile.

10

When I woke up the next morning to the sound of Russell's attempts at crowing, Chuck wasn't in his favorite spot, with his back to my shoulder and his head on the pillow next to mine. I sat up with a jolt; where was Chuck?

And where was the kitten?

The two had coexisted relatively peacefully that night; I had checked on the kitten frequently to feed her, per Tobias's instructions, and although Chuck sniffed at the box every time I got up, he always retreated to the bed with me.

I jumped out of bed and ran over to the box. It was empty.

My stomach dropped. Where was the kitten? And had Chuck done something to her while I'd slept?

"Chuck! Chuck!" I called as I sprinted down the hall, praying that nothing horrible had happened. I checked the kitchen, first... no sign of the poodle lying in his traditional spot near the oven, or nosing around the fridge. I ran into the living room next. The slipcovered couches were cat- and dog-free, as was the rocking chair I kept in the corner by the window for reading. As I was about to head outside and check the yard, I heard a tiny rumbling sound from near the fireplace.

I hurried toward the hearth. There, curled up on the edge of the rug, hidden by the end of the couch, was Chuck, looking up at me with his big brown eyes. Tucked up against his belly was the gray-and-white kitten, who now stretched out her little paws and yawned so big I could see her tonsils. As I watched, she began kneading Chuck's side with her tiny paws; although her tiny claws must have hurt, Chuck just turned and gave the kitten's head a rough lick, then put his head back down on the floor and waited patiently for her to finish.

"Wow," I said in a gentle voice. "You two are fast friends now." I bent down and stroked Chuck's head. "Did you keep her from going back up the chimney? If you did, you're a very good dog. In fact, you're a very good dog all the time." As the kitten settled back in, I made my way to the kitchen to make coffee... and get a little treat for Chuck.

A few minutes later, I padded back into the living room with my coffee mug in one hand and a little bit of fresh cheese in the other. "Not a word to Tobias," I warned Chuck as he gobbled the cheese. He gave me a panting smile and then gave the kitten another lick before settling back in. The kitten purred, but didn't open her eyes. I took my coffee to the bedroom, got dressed, and quietly headed out the back door to do the milking and gather eggs from the chickens.

If the damage to the chicken coop and the historic little house had really been the work of a vandal, they didn't appear to have made a return trip the previous night. The roof of the coop was still intact, and the restrung cables holding the house up were all still taut and unharmed. Ed and Nick had taken to locking the front and back doors of the little house, too; they were still shut tight, I was glad to see. In addition, all the cows and goats were accounted for.

The sun had inched well over the horizon as I headed back to the house with a basket of eggs and two buckets of milk. A cool breeze that foretold the coming autumn was sweeping over the pasture, ruffling the grass, and the air was perfumed with just the tiniest touch of woodsmoke. I was guessing someone had fired up the smoker for a brisket; it was still a tad warm for a fire in the fireplace, but all the same, the scent stirred up anticipation of cozy evenings by the fire.

I'd just put the eggs in a bowl in the fridge and poured the milk into a pot on the stove when Ed's truck bumped up the driveway. Chuck abandoned his role as cat bed and ran to the door, barking; a moment later, the kitten followed, stretching and yawning and looking completely unconcerned.

I waited until Ed parked to let Chuck out the front door. He raced over to the truck, greeting Ed as he swung down from the front seat. I made sure the kitten was still inside as I closed the door behind me and walked out to greet the contractor, who was dressed in neat blue jeans, his best boots, and a white button-down shirt. He was holding something that looked like a camera in his hand.

"What's that?" I asked.

"Security camera," he told me, bending down to scratch Chuck behind the ears. "Everything here doin' okay? No more monkey business?"

"Not that I saw," I told him.

"Well, if they do anythin' else, we'll catch 'em on this," he said, tapping the camera. "I just have to find a place to put it."

"Let me know if you need a hand," I said.

"I think I should be fine," he said. "Nick's comin' over later; I've got an interview in town."

"What for?"

"Biddin' on the Buttercup Bank job. Don't you worry, though. If we do get it, it won't start until after your little house is done."

"Well, then, I hope you get it."

"Me too," he said, but he didn't look hopeful.

"Who's the competition?"

"Oh, some bigwig firm out of Houston. Say they can do it in half the time for a third the money." He rolled his eyes. "Of course, I know that ain't the case, but you know how bankin' folks can be. All about return on investment and all that. Problem is, they don't know they've bought a pig in a poke until they're a year down the road and the project's only half done and twenty-five percent over budget."

"Surely your reputation around town will help?" I suggested.

"That's how things used to get done around here," he said. "But Buttercup Bank's part-owned by some folks out of the big city, so it could go either way."

"I'll be pulling for you," I said. "If you need a reference..."

"Even after the house almost fell down on Nick?" He gave me a wry smile.

"You and I both know that had nothing to do with you," I said.

"Yeah, well, Nick told everybody at the brewery what happened," he told me. "I got a call from his daddy, too. Told me I needed to keep a more watchful eye."

"Did you take pictures of the cables?"

"I should have," he said, "but I didn't." He sighed. "Things just ain't what they used to be around here."

"I'm sure you'll get the job," I said. "At any rate, I'm

looking forward to getting my project up and running. What all is left?"

"Once we get her stable, we're finishin' up the bathroom downstairs, puttin' in new counters and cabinets in the kitchen like we talked about, and slapping on some more paint."

"I ordered the appliances last week," I said. "Should I have waited?"

"If they get here early, we'll just keep 'em in boxes in the barn," Ed assured me. "Better to have 'em ahead of time than end up waitin' six weeks because some oven is on backorder."

"True," I said.

"Well," he said, "let me get this set up and then I've got to head into town. Nick should be here in a bit to finish replacin' some of the sheathin'. I'm hopin' we can get goin' on the kitchen by the end of next week."

"Counters came and cabinets are on the way," I said. "They should be here by Monday."

"Perfect timin'," he said, then tapped the camera in his hand. "I'll get this here camera set up and be on my way, but like I said, Nick'll be here soon." He squinted at me. "He doin' okay?"

"He seems to be working hard," I said.

"He's a good worker when he wants to be," Ed admitted, "but sometimes I think his mind wanders."

"He's a teenage boy," I said. "I think they're known for that. He seems like a good kid."

"A bit naive, but I suppose you're right," Ed said. "I just wish his daddy would get off his back. And mine." He sighed. "Oh, well. I guess I rode my kids hard, too. What goes around..."

I grinned at him. "Payback, eh?" I glanced down at

Chuck, who had deposited himself at Ed's feet and was looking up at him with a hopeful expression. "Oh—I found a kitten in my chimney last night, by the way. I think the mama cat is still hanging around somewhere—I saw her in the smokehouse last night. Seen any cats while you've been working?"

"I've seen one a few times; I thought it was yours. Gray stripy thing, skittish?"

"That's the one," I said. "Where have you seen her?"

"Near the chicken coop a couple of times," he said.

"Not too far from the smokehouse, then. Any sign of kittens?"

"Not that I saw, but I wasn't lookin'. Might want to ask Nick when he gets here."

"I will," I said. "Let me know if you see her again, or any kittens, okay?"

"Will do," he said, tipping his hat—he was actually wearing one made of straw—and then strode toward the Ulrich house, camera in his hand, with me in his wake.

"Part of the chicken coop roof was pried up last night," I told him. "I found a raccoon slipping out of the coop. I thought it might be him, but if someone's here vandalizing things... is there any way to tell?"

"Did you see any dents where someone might have used a crowbar, or a hammer?" he asked.

"No," I said, "but it was dark. I didn't look too closely."

"Hard to know," he said. "I'll take a look in a bit. In the meantime, I'd stay alert. Too bad you don't have a watch dog, or maybe some guineas."

I hadn't thought of adding guinea fowl to the farm. I'd seen the black and white-spotted birds with their crested, red heads more than once; the odd-looking creatures, native to Africa, had a reputation for adopting particular areas and guarding them fiercely, putting up a huge racket when anything came near.

"I've heard about them, but never thought about getting any," I said.

"One of them adopted Lenny Froehlich's '54 Ford pick-up a few years back," Ed said. "Made a kerfuffle every time he tried to get in and drive it to town. He finally gave up and had to get a Tacoma."

"Really?"

He nodded.. "Really."

"That's dedication." I stared at the little house, with its slightly crooked frame and its metal roof, and thought of its years of history. With everything else that had been going on, I'd kind of forgotten about the sabotage, but it made me uneasy. Uneasy enough to want to find a way to keep an eye on the place when I couldn't be there. "I wonder if I could get a small flock to adopt the house?"

"If you're thinking of rentin' it out, you might warn the tenants. They make a heckuva racket at sunset every night. And on that metal roof, they'd sound like they were tap-dancin'."

"That might be a problem," I said.

"I think a video camera might be a better call than guinea fowl. This one's got a motion sensor and everythin'."

"And if someone's trying to vandalize the place, maybe we'll be able to find out who."

"If someone's goin' after my jobs, I want to know, too. I don't know if it's you or me they're after, or if someone was just havin' their version of fun, but better safe than sorry."

"Can you help me set it up?"

"Sure thing," he said. "In fact, I'll put it up now."

"Everything still looking okay?" I asked.

"Yup. We fixed up the damage and we're back on track.

Hope to have you up and runnin' in time to rent it out during the antique fair in the spring; we're a little late for fall, but maybe in the new year?"

"That would be great," I said. "Thanks."

"My pleasure. I'll just go get this set up," he said, tapping the camera.

"I've got drinks in the house if you're thirsty," I said. "Help yourself; I'm going to be working here myself for the next few hours."

"Thank you, Ma'am," he said, and tipped his straw hat as he headed down to set up the camera.

I walked across the yard, Chuck at my heels, thinking about the mother cat. I didn't know if she could be tamed, but I wanted to find a way to get her spayed so that she didn't have another litter of kittens. Would a Have-A-Heart trap be the way to go? But what if she had other kittens hidden away somewhere, and wasn't able to get back to them?

I sighed as I stepped into the living room. The kitten had found her way to the rug in front of the stove and had curled up into a little gray ball. Chuck trotted over and began grooming her as I filled two bowls with cat food and water and put them on the back porch, just in case mama cat was hungry.

11

*T*he Oktoberfest market at the Town Hall didn't start until six in the evening, so I spent the rest of the day clearing more of the pumpkin and squash patch and making more goat milk flan. On the fifth try, I finally got the hang of the caramel, which made the process much faster. It turned out delicious, thank goodness, and I hoped it would sell well. Flan might not be German, but since there'd been an elotes stand at the brewery, I wasn't too worried about adding a bit of Mexican flair. Besides, diversification was the name of the game, right?

Nick turned up at around eleven. At noon, I took a break from making flan to head down to the house with a ginger ale.

"Any more near-catastrophes?" I asked as I handed him a ginger ale.

"Thanks," he said, wiping his brow with a blue bandana, and said, "Not so far. But I'm being extra-careful. My dad just about had a coronary when I told him what happened." He took a swig of ginger ale.

I spent the next hour doing kitchen work. Once I

finished tucking the last batch of the cooled flans into the fridge, I spent some time packaging more of my new Autumn Spice scented soaps, which I'd poured into leaf-shaped molds using soap in a variety of reds, golds, and oranges, into little mesh bags with handmade labels. I'd made them a while back; they'd been curing for weeks, and were ready to sell. As I put the last bag into the crate I used to carry them, I took an appreciative sniff; the mix of spices made for a delightful scent that made me excited about crisp fall nights, pumpkin pie, and cozy fires.

But it wasn't fall just yet, I reflected as I checked my inventory of flans and fresh goat cheese (some of which I'd rolled in fresh herbs this time). Then I set to work creating a sign advertising my "goat milk crème caramel" and dug out some sample spoons from my storage bin. When I was satisfied that everything inside the house was taken care of, I headed out to cut some flowers from the cutting garden I'd planted at the end of the yard. I spent a fun half hour creating beautiful bouquets of Mexican Bush Sage, zinnias, coral vine (which covered the fence to the west of the house in a glorious burst of pink), and fragrant Mexican Mint Marigold, adding in a few bits of fennel here and there. I sniffed the cheerful yellow flowers of the Mexican Mint Marigold as I finished another bouquet; I loved the flowering herb, which was not only beautiful, but a dead ringer for fresh tarragon in French-inspired dishes. Which was a very good thing, since tarragon is notoriously hard to keep alive in Texas's hot climate.

Once the flowers were all bundled into bouquets and nestled into a bucket of water, I loaded a box with a bolt of the blue-and-white-checked fabric I'd picked up in a fabric store in Austin, and several rolls of fairy lights to string around my booth. I grabbed a flat of rosemary plants, too;

I'd been nursing them through the summer, and hoped they would be popular. Fall was the best time to plant perennials in Texas, so that the cool fall and winter rains could help their roots grow deep and get established before the punishing summer began.

In between market prep chores, I made frequent stops to the bedroom to check on the kitten, feed her, and give her a few encouraging pets. Tobias and I had set up a temporary litter box for her, made out of an old cardboard peach crate and some cat litter that I kept in the barn for oil spills. The kitten was still sleeping a lot, but was always happy to see me, and was becoming more active after every feeding. I had been glad to see her energy returning as the day progressed; now, as I went in to check on her one last time before heading out to the market, she was attempting to climb the lace curtains framing the big window.

"You're trouble, aren't you?" I said, laughing as she gave me a startled look from her big green eyes and let out a scratchy meow. I was feeding her every few hours now; should I leave her here at home, or take her with me so I could check on her regularly?

As I detached her from the curtains, the kitten snuggled into my arms, purring strongly. I was glad she wasn't scared of me; although I felt bad for any other kittens who hadn't made it, it was a good thing we'd found this one so young. Tobias said that feral cats do best if they start interacting with humans sometime in the first four weeks.

"Want to come with me?" I asked.

She meowed as if she understood me. I smiled and stroked her head, then put her in the litter box.

"Hang on," I told her. "I'll be right back."

I headed to the storage shed to retrieve the carrier I'd bought when I adopted Chuck from the shelter. As I opened the shed door, I caught a flash of something down by the house. Nick had headed home a while ago, so it couldn't be him. Was my vandal back, in broad daylight? Or I had I caught a glimpse of the kitten's mother?

I tucked myself behind the door and peered down toward the house. Had I really seen something?

After another five minutes of watching, I saw nothing. I glanced at my watch; I needed to get moving if I was going to make it to the market in time to set up. I grabbed the carrier, closed the shed door, and headed back to the farmhouse. Part of me was tempted to go down and check out what I had seen, but fortunately the bigger, smarter part of me knew I was short on time and fairly ill-equipped to deal with potential intruders. Ed might have put the camera up, but I hadn't asked him how to use it.

I'd have to remedy that tomorrow.

It was almost five-thirty by the time I rolled up to the town square. Like the brewery, it had been decked out to look like a quaint Bavarian town, with lots of blue and white bunting, fairy lights, and festive stalls. The green in front of the courthouse had been turned into a beer garden, with long picnic tables covered in blue and white tablecloths, complete with little jars of local wildflowers in the middle. Mayor Niederberger had been working with the German Club to make Buttercup's events even more special; obviously it was working.

As I secured the legs of my pop-up and set up my table, I scanned the booths on the edge of the green. Despite yesterday's brouhaha, Sweetwater Brewery had a big booth, complete with professional-looking table set-ups and signage and several taps; a few booths down was Max Pfeiffer's much smaller booth, which featured a card table and a keg, along with a hand-lettered sign inviting festival-goers to "Try Fayette County's Oldest Beer." Which wasn't the most appealing invitation; he could use a little help in the marketing department. He was sitting on a card table chair a few feet behind the table, his arms crossed across his chest, looking... satisfied? The sun glinted off his scalp, which was peeking through his few remaining strands of hair.

My eyes drifted to the Sweetwater Brewery booth. There was no sign of Teena, but Simon was there, directing his workers as they set out cups and wired the price list to the top frame of the booth. His movements were jerky, and his face, usually animated and friendly, was devoid of expression. It must be hard to lose a brother, I thought. Particularly one with whom your life was so entwined. Although if Simon had been the responsible party, maybe it was the threat of jail that had him so upset? I didn't like to consider it, but I couldn't eliminate the possibility.

I checked on the kitten's water—she was tucked into the back of the carrier, watching everything with big green eyes—and then searched the gathering crowd for other familiar faces as I spread out the tablecloth and began arranging the autumn spice soap bags in a display basket. Adriana Janacek, the unfortunate barley farmer, didn't seem to be in attendance, but Ed was standing at Bubba's barbecue booth, wearing his trademark boots and jeans. I reminded myself to tell him to be extra-careful next time he and Nick were down at the house. I didn't know if I'd been imagining things or not earlier that day, but better safe than sorry.

I had just finished putting out samples of my flan and arranging the bouquets of flowers at the end of the table when Mandy Vargas appeared, a notebook in her hand and an eager look on her face.

"I tried to call you earlier, but there was no answer," she said.

"I've been pretty busy," I said. "I probably turned my ringer off and haven't checked for messages. It's been crazy getting ready for the festival."

"I understand you were there when they found Felix Gustafson," she said, her eyes glinting with the fervor of a journalist on a hot trail. I liked her, but there wasn't much I could do to help her with the story; I knew as much as everybody else.

"I was," I admitted.

"What did you see?" she asked, pencil poised over her notepad.

I shrugged as I rearranged the flowers. "They opened the big doors, and he was there on the floor, under a big bag of barley." I shuddered.

"Was anyone else in the brewery?"

"Not that I saw," I told her.

"But you saw Adriana Janacek at the festival."

"I did," I said. "Why?"

"She threatened Felix a couple of days ago at the Hitching Post," she said.

"Over the barley deal, right?"

"You know about that."

"The whole town knows about that," I said. "What did she say she'd do?"

"I'll tell you, but only if you promise to tell me first if you find out anything else."

"If it's something I can talk about, I will," I assured her.

"Okay. For your ears only. Felix was there with a little sample of his Dubbel Trouble, and Adriana was already on her sixth or seventh Cosmopolitan, according to Frank Poehler."

"Those do go down fast," I said. Frank was the bartender at the Hitching Post, and although he mainly slung beers, this being Buttercup, I knew he made a pretty mean craft cocktail, too. "But seven does seem excessive."

"Right," Mandy agreed. "Anyway, she got up and chucked the remains of Cosmopolitan #7 at him, then threw the glass on the floor. And then she said that if her business was going down, she'd make damn sure his went, too."

12

"*T*hat seems a bit... passionate," I said.

"I thought so too," Mandy said. "Do you know if they might have been seeing each other romantically?"

"Not that I've heard," I said, although it sounded like a possibility. What would Teena make of that if it were true? I wondered. Or had he broken up with Adriana to start dating Teena? All speculation, of course, but worth investigating. "So you're thinking Adriana might have been responsible for whatever happened to that barrel of beer."

"Maybe. Do you know anything about what happened?"

"Only that Teena marked the barrel they were going to use ahead of time," I told her, "and that when they opened it, it was off. It could be something wrong with the barrel, but Felix was known to be such a stickler that it doesn't seem likely."

"So assuming someone sabotaged it, anyone could have figured out which one to tamper with, if they were so inclined."

"Exactly," I said. "And I don't think the Gustafsons kept a

lock on the door. Nick Schmidt was back there, too, and he doesn't work for the brewery."

"Nick Schmidt?" I nodded as she wrote it down, then wished I hadn't mentioned seeing him. "Interesting. What was he doing back there?"

Looking for Teena, was my guess, but I wasn't going to tell Mandy that. "I don't know. I didn't talk to him about it."

"Do you think he might have had a motive for... well, for what happened?"

It was possible that Nick's crush on Teena might have led him to want Felix out of the way—after all, he'd seen them kissing that day—but again, I didn't feel right telling Mandy that. Nick hadn't told me he had a crush on Teena; I was just making an assumption. A well-founded assumption, but not anything I was willing to tell a reporter. "Not that I know of," I said, hoping I was right and that young Nick had had absolutely nothing to do with what had happened at Sweetwater Brewery that day.

She must have sensed my hesitation. "Are you sure?"

"I'm sure," I said firmly.

"So," she said, checking her notebook, "do you know anything about Max Pfeiffer?"

"Same as everyone else," I said. "That he was jealous of the Gustafson brothers' success."

"And he was suing them," she added. Then she gave me a sidelong look. "I heard some rumors about Felix Gustafson having a shady past."

"Oh?" I said. "What did you dig up?"

"I'm not sure," she said, "but he seems to have been involved in some trouble in the past."

"Like what?" I asked.

Before she could answer, Tobias walked up to the booth. "Hey," he said, surveying the display. "I was coming to see if you needed any help, but it looks great." His blue eyes spotted the carrier. "Is that the kitten?"

"It sure is," I told him. "I was afraid Chuck wouldn't let me take her with me; he's taken over the role of kitten parent. I found them all snuggled up in the living room this morning."

"That's great news," Tobias said. "I was worried Chuck might be a cat-chaser."

"Not so far," I said.

"She eating okay?" Tobias asked.

"She is, and seems to be quite alert," I reported as he opened the carrier and pulled out the little gray ball of fluff.

"She's adorable!" Mandy cooed. "Can I take a quick picture?"

"Sure!" I said, and Tobias assented to have his photo taken, the tiny kitten cradled in his hands. "That should sell some papers," Mandy said in a low voice, and I couldn't help grinning. "Anyway, I've got to go take pictures of the Buttercup Marching Band for the community page," Mandy continued. "Call me if you find anything else out!" she added, then hurried off toward the stage.

"What was that all about?" Tobias asked.

"She's writing an article on what happened," I told him.

"Does she have any new info?"

I readjusted the soaps and stood back to look at the table. "She told me Adriana threw her drink at Felix at the Hitching Post the other night."

"Over what?"

"Presumably the business, but we were wondering if there might have been something between Adriana and Felix." I adjusted the blue-and-white tablecloth a bit. "Have you heard anything?"

He shook his head. "No, but then again I'm not exactly

grapevine central. Quinn might have a better idea about that." He inspected the booth. "You did a great job with the booth, but where's your sign?"

I slapped my forehead. "Thanks for reminding me! Can you help me put it up?"

"Of course," he said as I hurried to the truck and pulled the rolled-up canvas sign out of the truck bed.

As we stretched the sign out across the top of the pop-up I used for shade and tied the sign to the posts, I turned back to my conversation with Mandy. "Anyway, she told me Max Pfeiffer was suing the Gustafsons, but I already knew that," I continued. "And she mentioned that Felix had a bit of a shady past—Flora said the same thing—but I still don't know the details."

"Shady?" Tobias cocked a dark eyebrow. "As in jail time?"

I finished tying off my side of the sign and stepped back. "Like I said, she just used the word 'shady.' That's all I know."

Tobias finished his side of the sign and brushed his hands together. "So she's thinking it might be someone from the past who killed him?"

"There were a ton of people at the brewery that day," I said. "It's possible."

"Did we ever find out who that woman was who was talking to Simon and Max the other day?"

"I'm guessing she's with a distributor or something, but no, I haven't heard anything."

"I'll ask around," Tobias said. As he spoke, the mayor's voice sounded on the microphone. "I think we're about to open," Tobias said.

"Sounds like it," I agreed as Mayor Niederberger launched into her opening remarks. "I was going to grab a bratwurst before I opened; would you mind going and getting one for me? I ran out of time to eat."

"I'll be right back," he said, and gave me a quick kiss. "Anything else? Maybe another Bluff lager?"

"That would be great. And maybe a gingerbread heart from the Blue Onion?" I asked. As I spoke, my eyes strayed to where Simon was standing, arms crossed, watching his booth. "Bonus points if you can find out anything interesting."

"I'll see what I can do," he said, and headed off on his mission.

THE NEXT FEW hours were so busy I hardly had time to think. The mayor and the committee workers had created a wonderful atmosphere, with several of the locals dressed in traditional German garb (think dirndls and lederhosen), and not one, but three separate oompah bands and the Buttercup Marching Band took the stage at various times. If I had thought the scene thoroughly German at the brewery opening yesterday, today I might have thought I was in Bavaria instead of Buttercup, even though most everyone spoke English, and there was more than the occasional pair of cowboy boots in evidence.

The cool September weather had brought throngs of people, and I sold about half the flans from the cooler (thank goodness) and almost all the soaps and candles I'd brought with me; it was a good market. Bessie Mae came by the booth, moving slowly but under her own steam using a walker—she'd been under the care of the whole town for many years now, and lived in a house right by the old train depot, where she loved to sit and watch the freight trains go by. She had been confined to a wheelchair last fall, and proceeds from our last Christmas Market had gone toward renovating the house to widen doorways and avoid steps so that she could stay in it. She seemed to be making progress, and when she fell in love with the autumn spice soaps, holding them up to her cute snub nose and cooing, I gave her a bag for free. I smiled as a look of delight crossed her face.

"For me?" she asked, with a childlike wonder that I often envied.

"For you," I confirmed, and as she tucked the soaps carefully into her bag and thanked me, I couldn't help but smile. Nobody was anonymous in Buttercup. We'd had a few run-ins with poison pen letters and feuds, but for the most part, the townspeople looked after each other. I loved that about this place.

As Bessie Mae pushed the walker toward the kettle corn booth a few stalls down, another horde of shoppers, well lubricated with Sweetwater Brewery's offerings, descended on my booth. One of the nice things about Oktoberfest (at least from a merchant's standpoint) is that the addition of beer seems to loosen the purse strings; it was turning out to be a very profitable venture for me. As I wrapped up yet another pair of beeswax candles, I sent a longing glance toward my dinner. Tobias had dropped off my food earlier, but I still hadn't had a chance to enjoy it.

Finally, the traffic slowed, and I took five minutes to sit down and eat. As I finished off my bratwurst and bit into the spicy gingerbread heart Tobias had picked up for me, I glanced over at the kitten, who had come to the front of her carrier when she scented the bratwurst. I was letting her lick my fingers with her rough tongue when Teena came up to the booth.

"Is that a kitten?" she asked. "It's so cute!"

"I found it in my chimney last night. I think her mom is

somewhere around the farm; we can't find any siblings, so we're taking care of her in the meantime."

"She's adorable. What's her name?"

"We haven't decided yet."

"Are you keeping her?"

"Haven't decided that yet, either," I said, although I kind of knew that wasn't true. Chuck was smitten with the little kitten, as was I... and besides, I'd been wanting to have a cat to scare off any mice who might brave the farmhouse kitchen. And was there anything better than reading with a cat in your lap? Except maybe reading with Chuck in your lap...

"How are you feeling?" I asked, turning my attention from the kitten to the young woman. Dark circles ringed her eyes, and her hair was lank around her young face.

"Awful," she said in a stricken voice. "I just can't believe he's gone."

"I know," I said. "It was so sudden."

"Horrible," she said. Her eyes looked at me, pleading. "Did you find out anything about who did it?"

"What? Why?"

"I just... I just have a feeling there's something hidden," she said. "And you're good at finding out the hidden things."

"Thank you," I said, and held up the cookie. "Want some?"

"Not really. I... I just can't eat much. My stomach is all twisted in knots."

"I understand," I said gently. "But what did you mean by 'hidden things'?"

She shrugged. "You know. The things other people don't want you to find out."

I'd never thought about it that way, but she wasn't

wrong. "Given any more thought to what 'repeating' means, by the way?"

"That's what I said when I passed out, right?" she asked.

I nodded.

She bit her lip and thought about it for a moment. "I don't know," she said. "Maybe something else will come. Sometimes it does."

I had a thought, then. Could I use Teena's psychic abilities to solve one of my own mysteries? "Just between you and me, I think someone vandalized the little house I moved down by the creek," I told her. "I put up a camera, but do you think you might be able to come up with some idea of who did it, and why, if you came by for a visit?"

"I don't know," she said. "I don't have any control over it, really, but being in places can sometimes bring up stuff for me. I can try if you want. But will you promise you'll keep looking into what happened to Felix?" Tears filled her eyes again.

"I will," I promised. "Is there anything you can tell me about him that might help?"

"Like what?" she asked.

"Like... was he angry with anyone? Do you know what was going on between him and his brother?"

"Well," Teena said, "Simon wanted to expand the business, make more money. Allow Felix's beer to be brewed in other breweries, so they could get more national distribution. Focus the brewery on the big sellers, including recipes from other breweries, and cut way back on the creative experimentation."

"And Felix didn't want to do that?

"Oh, Felix was all about creativity. About making the perfect beer. He didn't want to spend time making other people's recipes, and he sure didn't want other people brewing his beers... he wasn't convinced they'd be able to do them justice. He was livid about it."

"Mixing family and business can be hard," I said. "Did he ever talk about how the brewery was doing financially?"

"We didn't talk about it, really, but I know Simon was always super uptight about it. I think he handled the money side of things more than Felix. They argued about it, I know, but I don't know what was going on."

"Do you know the woman was Simon was talking with? Beth Collins?"

Teena nodded. "She's with Brewlific... the co-op distributor Simon wanted to sign with."

"Distributor, or co-op?" I asked, and took another bite of cookie.

"It's a co-op of big craft breweries across the country. They kind of act like a distributor, but they're not exactly the same. Close enough that Felix wanted no part of it, though."

"So the tasting was super important for the brewery in terms of signing on."

She nodded. "If they agreed to it, then Sweetwater Brewery would be brewing beers from other breweries across the country. Aside from what happened to Felix..." her face fell, and sadness washed across it again, "...it didn't look good yesterday. If we can't even get it right for a big reveal, then why would other brewers trust us with their beer?"

"I can see that," I said. "Do you have any idea what might have happened to that barrel Felix tapped?"

"Someone messed with it." She was vehement. "I'm sure of it."

13

"*W*ho?"

"It would make sense for it to be Felix, I suppose, but he would never do something like that." She thought about it for a moment. "I know Adriana Janacek was there. Maybe it was her, or Max Pfeiffer."

"What do you know about Adriana?"

She shrugged. "She seems out to get Simon, that's for sure. After the barley fiasco, I can see why she'd want to get back at Felix by embarrassing him in public."

"That was the only reason you know of?"

"What do you mean?" Teena narrowed her eyes at me. "Is there something else you know? I know Felix said he thought she had a crush on him once."

"Ah," I said. That would explain the incident at the Hitching Post. "Did they ever date?"

"Felix said she wasn't his type," Teena said. Since Teena was almost twenty years his junior, I was wondering if maybe Felix's type tended to significantly younger women, which frankly I found a little icky. Adriana was in her early thirties, only a few years younger than Felix.

"Do you still have access to the brewery?" I asked.

She nodded. "I've got keys," she said. "Why?"

"I think we should go take a look at the place," I suggested.

"Okay. When?"

"I don't want Simon to know we're there, necessarily. When would be a good time?"

"He left ten minutes ago. He's supposed to be in LaGrange for some kind of meeting tonight," she said. "Maybe after the market closes, we can go over?"

"Are you sure?"

"He usually spends the night in LaGrange when he goes," she told me in a low voice. "Felix told me he was seeing someone, but I don't know who."

"Teena!" one of the other employees called out. "We need help closing up!"

"Oh... sorry!" she called back. "I'd better get back to work," she said. "Meet me in a half hour? We'll go in my car, so it doesn't look suspicious."

"What will you say if someone asks about me?"

"We were going out for a drink," she said, "and I realized I left something behind at the brewery, so you came with me."

"Good enough, I suppose."

"I'm parked in front of the Red & White," she said. "See you in thirty."

As she headed back to the beer booth, Tobias returned to the stall.

"What was that all about?" he asked as Teena scuttled back to her post.

"Can you take the kitten back to the farm? I'm going over to the brewery with her tonight to look around," I told him.

He cocked an eyebrow. "Is that going to be okay with Simon?"

"He's not going to be there," I said.

"I don't like it."

"I know," I said. "But I promised Teena I'd help figure out what's going on. She doesn't think Simon is responsible for what happened to Felix."

Tobias sighed. "I know better than to try to talk you out of it, but I don't think you should do it."

"Noted," I said. "Now, will you help me pack the truck?"

TEENA WAS WAITING in her old Honda Civic when I headed over to the Red & White. Tobias was taking all my remaining wares back to the farmhouse in his truck; I'd follow once we finished at the brewery.

"Isn't it going to be busy with people putting things up?" I asked.

"They left with the kegs twenty minutes ago," Teena said. "By the time we get there, they should be all finished."

"How do you put up with that Billy person?" I asked as she drove.

"I can't stand him," she said. "I asked Felix to get rid of him, but he said he didn't have another good option for the job."

"Does he treat all the young women like he treats you?"

"A bit, but he mainly goes after me. I guess I'm just lucky that way," she said wryly.

"Billy said he's got all of Felix's recipes," I said. "Frankly, I'm not sure I'd trust him with them."

"Felix can't do all the brewing himself," Teena explained. "He has to delegate. But Billy was giving him a hard time about the recipes; he doesn't agree with Felix a lot of the time. Wants to do things his own way. Felix managed to keep him in check, though; he told me he's got talent."

"Talent's one thing," I replied, "but I don't trust him. And it bothers me that Felix kept someone around who treats you that way."

"I know," she said. "I hate it, too. And now, with Felix gone..."

"You're afraid he's going to step up the pressure?"

"Yeah. I might have to leave the brewery."

"I'd talk to Simon about it," I recommended.

"We'll see." She sighed, and we drove the rest of the way in silence.

She was almost right about the employees wrapping things up fast. When we rolled up the driveway, two of the employees were leaving the brewery and heading to their vehicles. I was glad to see no sign of Billy.

"Duck down," she said. "I'll go check and come back and get you when the coast is clear."

"Got it," I said, hunching down as she got out of the car.

I didn't have to wait long, fortunately; only five minutes later she was at the passenger door, motioning me to join her.

"All clear?"

"All clear," she assured me.

"No sign of Simon?"

"His truck isn't here," she said. "We're good."

I followed her across the parking lot to the front door of the brewery. Except for the lights strung around the picnic tables in the oak grove adjoining the brewery, there was no sign of the festivities that had taken place here yesterday.

Or the murder.

She took the keys out and unlocked the door; as she

opened it, cool, beer-scented air flowed out. She flipped on the overhead lights, illuminating the industrial-looking landscape of tall metal tanks, pipes, and complicated-looking machinery.

Teena's face paled as she turned to close the door behind us. "That's where it was..." she said, taking a deep breath and leading me to the large garage-style door where we'd found Felix just the day before.

Although there was no sign indicating the tragedy that had taken place here, we both still shuddered, remembering what had happened.

"How could the barley have fallen in the middle of the room like that?" I asked.

"It must have been suspended from here," she said, pointing to a track that led across the ceiling.

"Why would it be hanging there?"

"That's how it gets transported to where they pour it into the lauter tun," she said, pointing to a massive silver tank.

"What's a lauter tun?"

"That's where they mix the barley with hot water to make the wort."

Clearly there was a lot of vocabulary involved with beer-making that I knew nothing about. "What's wort?"

"Well," she said, moving into brewery tour mode, "you mix the water with the malted barley and heat it. The enzyme in the malt converts the starches into sugar, and the liquid that's left is called the wort. That's the first step in the beer making process."

"So someone was moving the barley from here—" I pointed to where multiple huge bags of barley rested "—to here, where it would be poured into that tank with water."

"Right," she said.

"But why would someone be doing that during Okto-berfest?"

Her young brow furrowed. "You know, I never thought about that. Everyone was out working the festival."

"How do you move it across?" I asked.

"It's up here," she told me, leading me to a narrow set of scaffolding-style stairs. I followed her up them to a metal platform. "I'm not sure exactly how it works," she said, pointing to a dashboard of sorts, "but you use this to hook the bag, and then you hit this button to transport it across to the lauter tun. Only... the cable's broken."

"You're right," I said. The heavy cable was coiled like a snake in the corner. I picked up one end; it was cut cleanly.

"Whoever did this didn't need to know how to operate the machinery, besides moving the barley bag back and forth," I said. "They just had to be able to lure Felix under the bag and then cut the cable."

"That's awful," she said, eyes wide.

"It is," I agreed.

"But the thing is," she said as we climbed back down the narrow stairs, "how would you get Felix to stop right under a giant bag of barley? I mean, that's crazy."

I thought back to the moment when the door opened and we saw Felix. "If it weren't for the cut cable, I'd think maybe it was an accident," I said.

"It wasn't," Teena said firmly. "I know that. I don't know why. I just do."

"Obviously you're right," I said, and closed my eyes, trying to remember the scene. "If I were trying to get someone to stop long enough for me to drop something on his head, I'd probably put something on the floor to make them pause where I wanted them to stand."

"There was a spilled beer on the floor near... near Felix,"
Teena said. "I saw it. It wasn't one of ours... that's why I noticed
it. I wondered why he was drinking a competitor's beer."

"Whose was it?"

"It was red and white," she said. "I think it's from Pfeiffer's brewery."

"That's the one Max Pfeiffer owns, right?"

"Right," she said.

"If I found a rival brewer's beer spilled on my brewery
floor just before a big opening, I'd stop to pick it up, too."

"But how did somebody get him here?" she asked.

"There was something in his hand," I remembered, my
eyes still closed. "It was on yellow paper."

"Well, good luck finding out about that," Teena said.
"Rooster will never tell you."

"No," I said, opening my eyes and staring at the spot on
the floor where Felix Gustafson had met his maker. "But I
know someone who might."

"Who?"

"Can't say," I said. "But let's look at the barrels before we
go. There might be a clue there."

"You think whoever killed Felix also tampered with the
beer barrel?"

"It could be," I suggested.

"Let's go look, then."

I followed her over to where several barrels stood,
stacked along a corrugated metal wall. There were two
empty spaces where the barrels from yesterday had been
moved, but the rest remained undisturbed.

"Where are these supposed to go, anyway?"

"They're destined for bars in Austin and Houston, mostly," she said. "And the tasting room here, of course."

"How would someone have tampered with a barrel, do you think?"

"Well, if Felix had opened it that morning, it wouldn't be too hard to re-open it and put something back into it."

"I know it was off—I saw the looks on their faces—but do you know what it tasted like?"

"Rotten eggs, is what Felix said."

"Ah," I said, scanning the floor around the barrels. It had been swept clean; but as I rounded the stack, I noticed a dusting of yellow on one of the lower barrels. I reached out and touched it with my fingertip, then raised my finger to my nose. "Ugh," I said. "I think I found the culprit."

"What is it?" she said, wrinkling her nose as I offered her a sniff.

"Sulfur," I said. "I've used it on the farm before."

"Gross," she said. "What do you use it for?"

"You can lower the soil pH with it," I said. "We sometimes have alkaline soil, so it helps, particularly with crops that like a little more acidity."

"Where do you get it?"

"Gardening stores. Hardware stores."

"So someone did tamper with the beer," she said. "I figured. The problem is, how do we find out who did it?"

"I might head down to Heinrich Feed and see if anyone's bought any lately," I told her. "They might sell it at the Red & White, too."

"Are they really going to remember someone buying a bag of sulfur?"

I shrugged. "You never know. The question is, did the same person who tampered with the barrel drop a bag on Felix?"

"How do we find out?" she asked, big eyes wide.

"I don't know," I said. "Maybe you could ask if anyone saw anything weird inside the brewery yesterday?"

"Weird like what?" she asked. As she spoke, there was the sound of tires on gravel. Even with the fans and machinery humming, it was unmistakable. Teena started like a frightened deer and ran over to the door, opening it slightly and peeking out. "It's him," she said as she peeked out.

"Who?"

"Simon. He's back early. Hide!"

———

14

"Quick... he's coming this way. You have to hide; you're not supposed to be in here," Teena said. I scurried away from the door and ran toward the massive brewing tanks lining the back of the building.

I'd just tucked myself out of sight when I heard Simon's voice. "What are you doing in here? Everyone's supposed to have gone home."

"I... I just was missing Felix," she said.

"Go home," he said sharply. "You're not supposed to be here."

"But..."

"Out," he snapped. "This is a dangerous place. You shouldn't be here alone."

"Yes sir," she said. A moment later, I heard the door close; I guessed Teena had followed orders and left the brewery.

With me still in it.

~

As I stood frozen behind one of the big tanks, I could hear

Simon moving around and muttering to himself. What would he say if he found me here? Why was he so adamant about Teena not being in the brewery?

And, I wondered, had he killed his brother?

"Mind her own business..." I heard him mumbling, along with some clanking. "Stupid stupid stupid. I had it all figured out, and then..." More loud noises. "Leave the business to me," he said. "None of this would have happened." I heard a few more clanks, and then the lights went out. A moment later, the door slammed shut. He was gone.

And I was locked in the brewery.

I waited quietly for several minutes before feeling in my pockets for my phone. Which evidently I'd left in Teena's car.

I said a few choice words under my breath, then crept out from behind the tank and edged toward where I hoped the door was. There was a little light from the tall windows, and that combined with the glow from the machinery displays was enough to make out major shapes, but I was still terrified of tripping over something dangerous.

Taking tiny steps, I edge over to the wall where the door was, and felt my way until I found the door frame. I reached for the doorknob; it turned, but nothing opened. My hands scrabbled at the door, searching for a deadbolt, but there was nothing. I pulled and pushed, but the door didn't budge.

I turned and tried to look for another exit. I remembered where the big overhead door was, and padded in that general direction, my hands out in front of me in case I ran into something. I had gone several yards when my hands encountered metal. It was one of the tanks. I felt my way around it to the wall; a little ways back the way I'd come was a panel. I'd found the big door.

I felt my way to the bottom until my hand closed on a handle. I pulled up, but nothing happened. I knew there was often a lock further up on the door, so felt my way around until I discovered a lever that felt like it might release the door, but apparently that was locked, too.

Defeated, I sank to the floor and gazed around the brewery, willing my eyes to adjust to the low light. Surely there must be an emergency exit in a place like this. It was a dangerous building; weren't there laws about that?

Unfortunately, no handy glowing EXIT signs presented themselves. After a few minutes, my eyes started to get used to the darkness; I could make out the shapes of the tanks, and even the corridors between them. I decided to do one more trip around the brewery floor before giving up and waiting for Teena to return.

Assuming she would return.

She would, right? Even if she had to walk down the driveway to avoid alerting Simon?

After a trip around the brewery floor, I resolved to talk to the mayor about improving code regulations in Buttercup—I'd found one more door, but it was also locked—and sat down on the floor by one of the big tanks in the back.

The sound of all the whirring, rumbling machinery was soothing. As I sat, my back against one of the metal tanks, I could feel my mind sorting through all the things I'd learned. A spilled beer on the floor by the body. Adriana throwing her glass at Felix at the Hitching Post. Felix's supposed shady past. The rival brewer with the lawsuit. The cash-strapped brother Simon, who'd been muttering like a madman just a few minutes ago, and hadn't wanted Teena here. And Nick, with his fascination with Teena. So many possibilities, and only one of them was the culprit.

Was it Simon, or one of the other people who had a beef with Felix?

Or was I missing something entirely?

My nose started hurting... almost a burning sensation. I didn't smell anything weird, but I reached in my pocket and pulled out a crumpled napkin from earlier in the evening. I blew my nose, but it didn't seem to help. I did, however, have the urge to lie down. My first instinct was that I should stay alert, but really, what were the odds that Simon would come back to the brewery? And if Teena came back, surely she'd know there was no way out, so she'd search for me.

After a moment of indecision, I lay down on the cool floor, using my upper arm as a pillow. The machinery almost sounded like a symphony now, or like a white noise machine, or maybe even the ocean...

I closed my eyes, feeling the vibration through the floor. I was so sleepy. Maybe I'd just take a quick nap before Teena returned...

"Lucy. Lucy!"

The words seemed to be coming from a distance. I was vaguely aware of someone shaking my arm. I batted it away; it was bothering me.

"Get up! Now! You should never lie on the floor in a brewery!"

"What?" I asked, groggy.

"Carbon dioxide poisoning." It was Teena's voice. "I have to get you out of here. Can you stand?"

"Carbon what?"

"You don't have enough oxygen in your brain. Now, get up!"

She helped me to my feet. The room was still dark... or was it? I couldn't tell anymore. I remember falling once or twice, and a door opening, and then sucking in big breaths of clean air.

"Let's get to the car," she whispered urgently. "Come on!"

By the time we got to her Honda Civic, which she'd parked a way down the driveway, I was feeling more cogent.

"Oh, man," I said, once things stopped being so muddled. "What happened?"

"Shh... let's talk about it in the car," she said. "I know we're far from the house, but I don't want to take chances."

"Got it," I told her, glancing up the driveway toward the house. The lights were on, and there were two trucks in the parking spots on the side of the building; Simon must still be home.

I waited until she'd turned the car around and had gotten far enough from the house to feel comfortable turning on the headlights before I asked what had happened.

"Did you fall, or did you see anyone else who might have hit you over the head or something?"

"No," I said. "I mean, other than Simon. But he didn't see me."

"So you didn't hit your head. And you didn't take any drugs or anything, right?"

"Of course not!" I said.

She sighed. "The ventilation must not be working right."

"That's a problem?"

"A big problem; I'm going to have to make sure someone looks at it, although I don't know why they'd listen to me."

"What's the issue?"

"The fermentation process makes a lot of carbon dioxide; it's heavy, so it sinks. I'm guessing you got carbon dioxide poisoning; some brewers have died of it in other places."

"I had no idea brewing beer was so dangerous," I said.

She looked sidelong at me. "My boyfriend just got crushed by a sack of barley. And there are forklifts and giant barrels all over the place. It's a minefield."

"Have there been a lot of accidents?"

"One or two," she said. "Nothing major."

"What were they?" I asked as she turned back toward town and my ability to string together sentences returned.

"Just a few things here and there," she said. "Nothing to worry about."

Try as I might, she wouldn't tell me anything else. I called Tobias and told him what happened.

"Are you okay?"

"I'm fine," I told him.

"I'll meet you at the square and decide that for myself," he said. "I knew going to the brewery was a bad idea."

I sighed. If I never did anything risky, I'd never find anything out. And so far, I still hadn't managed to die.

Not yet, anyway.

TOBIAS WAS WAITING by my truck when Teena dropped me off at the square.

"I took everything to the farm and came back here." He peered at my face. "You don't look so good. Did everything go okay?"

"I had a bit of a carbon dioxide issue, but other than that I'm fine."

"What?"

I told him what had happened.

"Lucy! I knew you shouldn't have gone. Are you sure you're okay to drive?" he asked.

"I'm fine," I told him. "I promise."

"I'm following you home," he said. "Just in case."

"That's kind, but I think I'm okay..."

"Stop arguing and get in the truck," he said. "And be careful."

The trip back to the farm was uneventful, and I admit it was comforting having Tobias behind me. As I turned up the driveway, though, my headlights flashed across the front of the Ulrich house.

The front porch had caved in.

I parked the truck and got out just as Tobias parked beside me.

"Something's wrong with the Ulrich house," I told him.

"What?" He grabbed a flashlight from the back of his truck. "Let's go take a look."

As we got closer to the little house, it became apparent that the two members holding up the porch roof had fallen over.

"Ed just replaced these," I said as we stood next to the crumpled roof. "What the heck is going on?"

"Maybe he didn't set them properly?" Tobias suggested, training the flashlight on one of the posts. "Look. The nails just got ripped out of the wood."

"How could that happen?" I asked. "Was the roof too heavy?"

"I don't think so." He turned to look at me. "I think somebody's sabotaging your project, Lucy."

~

"Why?" I asked.

"I don't know," he said.

I bit my lip. "Ed put in a camera. Maybe he caught whatever happened on film."

"Where is it?" he asked.

"I don't know," I said. "I didn't watch him put it up."

Tobias flashed the light around the perimeter. "I don't see it," he said.

"I'll ask him," I said, and pulled out my phone. It was a little late, but I knew Ed would want to know what had happened, so I called him. He didn't answer, so I left a voice mail. "This project is never going to be done, is it?" I asked.

"I'm less worried about the project and more worried that someone's got a vendetta against you. Or at least this house. Let's go check on the animals and the farmhouse and make sure whoever it was didn't get up to any more mischief."

We did the rounds of the farm; fortunately, the damage seemed limited to the Ulrich house. But I still didn't understand why.

"It makes no sense," I said. "Why attack my project?"

"Ed's up for the Buttercup Bank project," Tobias suggested. "Maybe somebody's trying to cause trouble with his existing projects so that he doesn't look like a good contractor."

"He did mention some of his concrete forms being trampled the other day," I said. "Maybe you're right. Maybe I'm not the target."

"Maybe not," he said, "but I still want you to be careful. Are you okay staying with me for a few days?"

"I really can't, not with all the chores here," I said.

"Are you okay with me staying here, then?" he asked.

"Yes," I said, and hugged him. "Thank you."

"Any time," he said. "I'll sleep better, too, knowing you're not alone."

THE NIGHT PASSED UNEVENTFULLY, and it was nice to wake up in Tobias's strong arms. I made coffee for both of us, and then we parted to take care of our morning duties. Chuck and the kitten were still getting along famously, and before heading out to his truck, Tobias proclaimed the little cat healthy and thriving, and reminded me she still needed frequent feeding.

After my morning chores, I headed to the Heinrich's Feed store to pick up food for the chickens, goats, and cows; I was getting low.

As Lotte Heinrich wheeled a few of the big propylene bags of cattle and goat feed out of the storage room on a dolly, I noticed the color was a little different. "It seems darker than usual," I said.

"We're goin' local," she said as I hefted a bag of chicken feed onto the counter. "Changin' it up a bit and tryin' to support local farmers. Speaking of local farmers, how's everything going at Dewberry Farm?"

"Getting the hang of things, I think. I lost all my cucurbits to bugs this week, but other than that it's all good," I said as she rang up my purchases. I loved the feed store; in spring, they had baby chicks in a special room, and all kinds of things—including poultry nipples and sheep tights—I had never even imagined you could buy. (Poultry nipples are things you put on buckets so that chickens can drink out of them, and sheep tights keep fleece clean, in case you were wondering.)

"None of your livestock gettin' sick?" she asked.

"No. Why?"

"We've had a lot of ranchers with sick cattle lately," she

said. "We've been wonderin' if there's some kind of fever sweeping through town."

"Tobias has had a few calls," I said. "What are you seeing?"

"Lameness is the big thing," she said. "I wonder if it's some mosquito-borne thing, like West Nile virus or something." She shivered. "You just never know these days."

"I know he's seen some lame cattle," I said as I gave her my credit card. That certainly was the issue with the Froehlichs' cows.

"Need help getting this to the truck?" she asked.

"That would be great," I said. I don't know why, but I suddenly asked, "Can I return it?"

She blinked at me. "Why on earth would you want to do that?"

"I don't know," I said. "In case Tobias wants me to change up their diets or something, I guess."

She shrugged. "As long as it hasn't been opened, I can't see why not." She accompanied me out to the truck. "Max Pfeiffer was in here earlier buyin' chicken feed and crowin' about some new deal he's puttin' together with a beer distributor," she said. "I heard you were there when they found Felix."

"I was," I said. "Hey... do you remember if anyone bought sulfur recently?"

"That's usually a spring kind of thing, that you till in. Don't have much call for it this time of year. I don't remember seein' any, but... hey, Missy!" she called across the store to a young woman with blonde pigtails.

"What's up?"

"You remember sellin' any sulfur lately?"

"Yeah, actually." She turned pink. "Just a few days ago.

Nick Schmidt came in for a bag; said his dad asked him to pick it up for him."

"Thanks, Missy." She turned to me. "She always remembers the cute college-age boys. Well, then," she said. "There you go."

"Do the Schmidts farm?" I asked.

"I know Nick's mom has a tomato patch. Maybe that was what it was for. Although she usually uses Epsom salts."

"Me too," I said.

At least I'd solved one mystery, I thought as Lotte helped me load the bags into the car.

Nick had almost certainly fouled the beer barrel before the big opening.

But was he responsible for what had happened to Felix, too?

I HAD GOTTEN BACK to the farm and was about to make another batch of mozzarella cheese when Tobias called.

"How are you? Still no aftereffects from last night?"

"Fine," I said.

"Sure?"

"Positive," I told him. I told him what I'd learned about Nick buying sulfur.

"So we've figured out the likely culprit for that, anyway... but it still doesn't solve the issue of who killed Felix.

Any word from Ed?"

"Not yet," I said, "and I still can't find the camera." I'd walked around the house before milking the cows and goats, wondering if I'd be able to locate it, but I'd been out of luck.

"I'm sure he'll know where it is."

"I just wish he'd call back." I looked down to where the little gray fluff ball was stalking Chuck's wagging tail. As I watched, she pounced on it, and Chuck jumped and let out a yip. "The kitten's playing the part of the mighty hunter this morning. Unfortunately for Chuck, his tail is the prey."

"He's been very patient, hasn't he?"

"He tolerates anything from her," I said. "He must have more holes in him than a pincushion after the way she was kneading his belly this morning. She thinks he's her mom."

"That's great news. No sign of the real mama today?"

"I may have caught a glimpse of her yesterday, but that's it," I said.

"I'm sure she'll turn up," he said. "I wanted to let you know I've got a call at the Janaceks' farm. I've got to look at some sick cows; you want to come with me?"

I looked at the milk in the pot, then out to the field of squashed squash plants I wanted to finish dealing with. I had lots to do. But I was dying to talk with Adriana.

"Absolutely," I said.

"I'll be there in ten minutes," he said, then hesitated. "You're sure you're feeling okay today?"

"No problems at all," I reassured him.

"Good. See you soon!"

I put the milk in the fridge for later and went to brush my teeth (I hadn't gotten there yet) and make sure I didn't have dirt all over my face or hay stuck to my head. By the time Tobias's truck rolled up the driveway, I'd gotten most of the straw out of my hair and looked somewhat presentable.

He greeted me with a kiss as I hopped into the truck. Chuck watched me from the window, looking sad that he wasn't invited to join us. Beside him, batting at the curtains, was the kitten.

"They do look happy," Tobias said, nodding toward the furry duo.

"They do," I agreed. "So, what's going on at Adriana's?"

"Several lame cows," he said.

"I'm guessing they didn't all twist their legs," I said.

He grinned at me. "That's a pretty safe assumption."

"I didn't know she ran cattle."

"She has a few head," he said. "The last thing she needs is for something to go wrong with them, after what happened with her barley gamble."

"Farming is risky," I said, thinking of my decimated cucurbit crops. "I'm glad I've got a lot of things going on. Which reminds me, I need to drop some veggies by the Blue Onion later on today. Although Quinn's going to have to buy her cucumbers from someone else, I'm afraid."

"Good thing those soaps sold so well," he said as he turned in at a stone gate that looked like it had been there since the dawn of time. Or at least the dawn of Buttercup.

We drove up a long, straight drive to a ranch-style house that did not come from the dawn of time, but rather the dawn of the 1950s, complete with dirty white brick and peeling pink shutters that must once have been cheerful. The front beds were filled with trampled dead grass and weeds, and the concrete walk was cracked.

"A bit of deferred maintenance, it looks like."

"You think?" Tobias said wryly. We got out of the truck, and once he grabbed his bag from the back, together we picked our way up the overgrown front walk to the door. He rang the bell; a minute later the faded blue door opened, and Adriana stood there, her dark hair caught up in a sloppy bun, dark circles under her eyes, and something of a wild look on her face. She wore an oversized A&M T-shirt that hung on her wiry frame, and faded jeans that had ragged holes in the knees—the kind you earn, not the kind you buy. "Thank you so much for coming," she said. "They're out in the barn. Follow me."

We waited as she pulled on her boots, and then together we headed to the weathered barn tucked behind a cluster of trees a little way back from the house. "In here," she said as she pulled the barn doors open.

We walked inside the dark, dusty barn, which smelled of animals and old grease and hay and dust and a hundred years of work. It took a moment for my eyes to adjust to the dim light; when they did, I immediately spotted the cows in question. They huddled in a corner together. As I watched, one took a small step and staggered a little, then seemed to regain its balance.

"How long has this been going on?" Tobias asked.

"I noticed the first one a few days ago. I thought she'd just stepped in a hole or something. But now all four of them are lame."

"Any other symptoms?"

"They're off their feed," she said.

"What are they eating?"

"They're out to pasture most of the day," she said. "I also give them some of this." She pointed to a bag of cattle feed; I recognized it as coming from Heinrich's.

"How long have you been feeding them this?"

"I always feed them this," she said, but her eyes darted around as if she was uncomfortable with the question. Had she been adding something to the feed? I wondered. "Why?"

"Just trying to locate the source of the ailment," he said. "Can I see some of it?"

"Sure," she said, and pointed him in the direction of an open bag in the corner. "It's all ground up," she said.

"What are these black flecks?" he asked, taking a handful of grain and running it through his hands.

She shrugged. "Just part of the grain, I guess. It was there when I opened it. Do you really think it's the feed, though? I mean, they're lame."

"I'm not sure what's going on," he said. "I'll take a look, though." As he examined the cows, I examined Adriana.

"I heard Sweetwater Brewery reneged on a deal with you," I said, leaning against an ancient post.

She nodded shortly. "Just about bankrupted me," she said, then gestured toward the cows. "And now this." She sighed. "It hasn't been my year, I'll say that."

It hadn't been for Felix Gustafson, either.

Was Adriana part of that?

15

"*Y*our family's been here a long time, haven't they?" I asked Adriana, who looked like—as the locals liked to say—she'd been rode hard and put up wet.

"Since almost the very beginning," she said. "The old house burned down in the early 50s, and my grandparents rebuilt, but we've been on this land since the mid-1800s." She untwisted her curly hair, playing with it nervously. "I'll never be able to forgive myself if I'm the reason it goes under. I never should have believed Felix, but he talked such a good game..." She looked up at me guiltily, as if she'd forgotten he was gone for a moment. "God rest his soul, of course."

"Of course," I said. "What happened, if you don't mind my asking?"

She sighed. "He sweet-talked me into dedicating three-quarters of the farm to some new barley that was supposed to grow well in warm-weather climates. Said we'd get it malted at some place up in Dallas and the brewery would buy the whole lot at a premium, because it was local. He was going to make some all-Texas beer... had someone growing hops, too, I hear." She took a deep breath. "So I planted everything, followed all the recommendations. We had a wet winter, as you know, but the harvest looked pretty good. And then he had it tested and told me..." Her hands clenched so that the knuckles turned white, and she took another deep breath. "Told me that it 'didn't meet their quality standards.' Can you believe it?"

"That's awful," I said.

"I know. I dedicated almost my entire farm to it, and he didn't buy a single bushel."

"What did you do?"

She looked miserable. "I sold it where I could," she said. "For pennies on the dollars he promised me."

Before I could ask more, Tobias spoke up. "They're sick, all right. I'm not sure with what, though."

She twisted her hair back up in a bun. "How will you find out?"

"I have an idea, but I have to get it checked out first," he told her. "I'd like to take a sample of your feed."

"Why would the feed make them lame? That makes no sense at all."

"There could be something wrong with the feed," he said calmly. "Where did you get it?"

"Like I said, Heinrich's Feed Store," she said, "just like everybody else. I always get the best local stuff; it can't be that."

"Maybe not. Can I take a look around?"

"I don't know what you'll find, but sure," she said.

Together we walked after him as he walked around inspecting farm equipment and even the stock pond.

"Shame about what happened to Felix Gustafson yesterday," I said.

"It is," she said. "I was mad, but..." Tears filled her eyes. She swiped at them with the back of her hand. "I'm sorry. We... we kept it quiet, but we were seeing each other for a while some months back. We made the deal while we were together, but he didn't want Simon to know, or else he'd accuse Felix of making a bad business deal."

"I can see that," I said.

"Anyway... a few months ago, I guess he started seeing one of the young women who works for him, and he broke it off with me. And then two weeks later he sends me a text message telling me he's not going to buy my barley."

"That's horrible," I said.

"Isn't it? I feel like he was just using me," she said. "Or trying to make my life miserable. I'm not saying I'm glad he's dead, but... he wasn't a very nice man."

"I heard there was some talk of embezzlement or something in his past?"

"I heard that, too," she said. "He told me it was the brewery owner who was cooking the books and then fingered him when he got caught. I believed it at the time, but now..."

"I can see that," I said. "What was the name of the brewery?"

She gave me a sharp look. "Why are you so interested?"

"Well," I said, "Our sheriff doesn't have a very good track record with arrests. A friend is worried Simon is going to go to jail for killing his brother. She's not convinced he's guilty."

Adriana nodded. "I can see that," she said. "Simon was a pretty hard-nosed businessman, but he loved Felix. I can't see him doing something like that to his brother."

"Even if they were up against the ropes financially?"

She blinked. "What? They looked like they were doing a booming business."

"I'm just speculating," I said. "It could explain why they didn't buy the barley."

"So it could be that it wasn't because it was not 'up to snuff?'" She thought about that for a moment. "If he'd just told me, we could have worked something out." Then her face darkened. "There's still that girl he started seeing."

"Did he do that while you were dating?"

"He says he didn't, but I know better," Adriana said. "He's such a wuss. Or was such a wuss." Tears filled her eye suddenly. "I don't know what to think. I'm still madder than a wet hen, but I also miss the good times we had... and I didn't think he was a bad person. Weak, maybe, but not bad."

"Weak?" I asked. "That surprises me. He was pretty firm about the direction he wanted the brewery to go."

Adriana waved me away. "Simon always got what he wanted." She eyed me directly. "Always."

"But he was generous, too, right?" I asked. "I mean, he wasn't the brewer of the family."

"True," she said. "But he's a salesman, not a creator. Felix, for all his faults, was a creator. Without Felix, Simon didn't have anything to sell."

"And now Felix is gone."

"Yes," she said. "But the brewery has a reputation. And Simon's got his brother's recipes to work from. And besides, Felix was starting to become a problem for the business."

"Problem?"

"Scotching deals," she said. "Simon was talking with an investor when I was dating Felix, and Felix just scared her off. Said that outside money would dilute control or something like that. And I heard Simon was looking into being part of some big conglomerate, so they could distribute nationally."

"I heard that too," I said. "Is it possible Simon thought Felix was too much trouble?"

She hesitated, and said. "I didn't think so, but... I just don't know." She ran her hands through her hair. "This is all just so upsetting."

"I know," I told her. "I was kind of surprised to see you at the brewery, to be honest. I heard you and Felix had a run-in at the Hitching Post."

She sighed. "I was drowning my sorrows. He came in with Teena, and I just... I was just upset." Her face reddened. "It's been a tough year. I haven't always handled it well. To be honest, I went to the brewery to kind of extend an olive branch."

"Oh, yeah?"

She nodded. "I was going to apologize for being so rude. Of course, I'm still furious about the barley thing," she said. "And the younger girlfriend. So... really. I don't know what I was doing there." The tears started again. "Maybe I just missed him."

"I get that," I told her. I glanced over at Tobias; I could tell he had finished his examination some time ago, but was giving me time to ask questions. I smiled a quick thank you and turned back to Adriana. "Can you think of anyone else in town who might have wished Felix ill?"

"He mouthed off a lot," she said. "Particularly when you got a few beers in him. Like I said, he was a weak man, but he liked to talk a big game."

"Who did he mouth off to, that you remember?"

"Max Pfeiffer, for one. Told him his beer tasted like... well, you know. Animal urine. Only in more colorful terms."

"Nice," I said. "When was that?"

"Oh, it happened more than once. Max would come up and start haranguing him about stealing the Pfeiffer Brewery's trademark, even though Simon figured out how to do it legally, and then Felix would get fed up and start talking back. Frank had to escort Max out of the bar one day. He hit Felix in the nose."

"Really?"

She nodded. "And some of the old-timers in town didn't take much to him, either. I know Max said more than once that Felix was all hat and no cattle, and wouldn't know a good beer if it bit him in the you-know-what."

"Got it," I said.

"It doesn't help that Max lives right down the road and gets tired of hearing all the cars and the noise from the beer garden."

"He was at the brewery the night Felix died, wasn't he?"

"I saw him by the pretzel stand," she said.

I made a mental note to go and find him if I had a chance. "Did Felix date anyone else that you know of?"

"He didn't talk much about his exes, to be honest. And they haven't been in town that long. They moved here just over a year ago, I think, but the brewery's only been open for six months or so."

"So no ex-girlfriends, or other troubles that you know of."

"No, but I know Simon got him out of a few scrapes in the past. Like I said, Felix gave Simon something to sell, but I also think Simon was trying to help his brother out. Which is why he was so mad when he felt like Felix was throwing it back in his face, I'm guessing."

"Scrapes?" I asked. "What kind of scrapes?"

She shrugged, and her eyes darted away from me. "Bad judgment stuff, I think."

"Bad judgment? Like..."

"I don't know," she said. "Financial stuff." She turned to Tobias. "What do you think?"

He grimaced. "Weight loss, coats are a little rough... some swelling in the joints... they're obviously not doing well, but I don't know what the cause is. Have you noticed anything else?"

"They hang out in the shade a lot more than usual," she said. "And it's not that hot out."

"To be honest, I've never seen anything quite like it. I don't know what to think." He bit his lip. "Can I take a look at your pasture?"

"What are you looking for?" she asked.

"I'm not sure," he said. "I just want to cover all my bases." Together we headed out to the pasture, which was a relatively small portion of Adriana's holding, the rest being given over to farmland, most of which appeared to be planted in beans.

The pasture, unfortunately, looked fairly hard-used; there wasn't much of it, and what there was was cropped practically down to the ground. There were several stands of prickly pear cactus, along with some bunches of thistles, but not a lot of anything else.

"Grass is pretty shot," she said. "We rely on hay and feed mostly; it costs a lot, though. I'm thinking I might make some of my own hay going forward."

"I see your beans are looking good, at least," I said, glancing over at the rows of dark green leaves. "Good for the soil, too. What are you planting this winter?"

"Wheat, probably," she said. "But I'm not going to bother trying to sell it to Sweetwater."

"I can see that," I said.

"I thought about goat farming," she said, "but evidently I

can't even keep cows alive, so why bother trying?" Her shoulders sagged.

"Goats do well in this part of the world," I said. "I know your family's been in the farming business for more than a hundred years, and you probably know more than I do, but if there's anything I can do to help..."

"Thanks," she said. "That barley really messed me up. I shouldn't have gone all in on it, but the price he was promising me..."

"Why wouldn't he accept it, again?"

"He said the quality wasn't there," she said. "He said he had a bunch of other brewers lined up, too, but that all evaporated once he decided the barley wasn't good enough."

"Sounds like you took a big hit, then."

"I did. Something's better than nothing, but it wasn't enough to cover my costs."

"I hope the coming year's a better year," I told her.

"Yeah," she said morosely, but looked back at the barn. "Not shaping up too well so far, is it?"

"They're still kicking," Tobias said, bending down to inspect some grass. "I'd like to change feed, but I know that's an extra expense. And if I could take some with me..."

"You think it's the feed?"

"I have no idea what it is," Tobias said, "but I'd like to start with that, if you don't mind."

"Sure," she said, swallowing. "How much do you need?"

"If you have a baggie, I'll just grab a cup or so. I'm going to take some hay and some grass from the pasture, too, and get all of it analyzed."

"How much will that cost?"

"Nominal cost," he said, waving her concern away. "Don't worry about it."

"Are you sure?" she asked.

He nodded. "I'll take a few samples from the cows, too."

"What should I do in the meantime?"

"Keep them in here," he told her. "I'd consider switching feed if you can manage it. I don't know if that's what it is, but I don't want to take chances."

"If that's what you think," she said. "I'll go get some other feed tomorrow."

"I'll leave a few medications for you to give them. Let me know how they're doing," he said, "and tell me if they get worse."

"I will," she said. "Thanks for coming out. Do you think they'll be okay?"

"I'm going to do everything I can to make it that way," he said. "Give me a call tomorrow, and let me know at once if things get worse."

"Thanks so much for coming out, Dr. Brandt," she said. "With everything else that's gone on... if I lose these guys, it could be the end of my family's farm."

"Then let's try to keep that from happening," he said.

"I'll go get some baggies," she told him. "Be right back."

"We'll be here," he told her.

As she hurried back to the house, her hair flying in the breeze, I turned to Tobias. "What do you think it is?"

"I have a suspicion, but I want to be sure first."

"Are the cows going to be okay?"

"If I'm right, and she does what I tell her to, I'm hopeful. But time will tell."

Tobias dropped me back off at the farmhouse a half hour later. I was just about to tackle the cheese again when the phone rang; it was Quinn.

"Did you hear what happened?" she asked.

I gripped the phone. "No. What?"

"Simon's been arrested."

"Oh, no," I said.

"And that's not all. You know that job Ed's been doing just west of town? The couple from Houston who's building that big modern farmhouse?"

"He said something about having trouble with a foundation there the other day. What about it?"

"Some of the scaffolding collapsed this morning, and Nick broke his leg."

16

"*I*s Nick going to be okay?" I asked.

"It's just the leg, so I'm sure it'll be fine," she said.

"Someone messed with the Ulrich house last night, too, I think... knocked down the porch roof. Do you think maybe the same person sabotaged the scaffolding at the other project?"

"I'd say talk to Rooster about it, but good luck with that. It's a reasonable theory, though."

"And what about Simon?" I asked. "How is the brewery going to go on with both of the partners gone?"

"Not just that, but the assistant brewer seems to have skipped town."

"That Billy guy?" I asked. "I didn't like him; I'm glad he's gone."

"Yeah, well, he was the only one who had Felix's recipes. And now they're gone, too."

"Poor Sweetwater," I said. "What are they going to do?"

"I don't know," she said.

"And poor Simon, too."

"Do you really think he did in his brother?"

"No," I said. "I know they argued, but part of the reason he started the brewery, from what I hear, may have been to give his brother a second chance."

"Which it seems he was willing to squander, taking both of them down."

"Maybe," I said. "But I think there's something else going on here. I just wish I knew what."

THE OKTOBERFEST MARKET was booming again that night; I found myself regretting that I hadn't spent more time making things to sell, and resolved to come up with a few more things to offer next year.

This time, I'd left the kitten home with Chuck; when I left, the two of them were sprawled out on the couch. Chuck was patiently allowing the kitten to stalk his tail, interrupting only occasionally to groom her. Tobias called to let me know he had several after-hours calls and would make it if he could.

"What's going on?"

"Sick cattle everywhere," he said.

"That's what Lotte at Heinrich Feed said." I glanced up at the throng of people at the booth. "Shoot... I've gotta run... I'll check in later."

I hung up and greeted the next set of customers, who were holding beers and examining my beeswax candles with interest.

The chocolate-dipped lebkuchen went in the first half hour, and the soaps and candles were flying off the shelves, but even as I packaged up goods and added up purchases, I found myself scanning the crowd—and the front door of the

Country Place Hotel—looking for Beth Collins, aka Bethany Jackson.

As I was doing another sweep of the crowd, Teena came up to the stall.

"Did you find anything out?" she asked.

"Not yet," I said, "but I have some leads." As I spoke, I spotted a dark-haired woman in tailored slacks getting out of an Audi and walking up to the front door of the hotel— Beth Collins, aka Bethany Jackson. "Hey," I said to Teena. "Can you man the stall for a few? I've got someone I need to talk to."

Teena blinked. "Sure," she said. "What do I do?"

"Price tags are on the merchandise. Use the credit card reader," I said, shoving it at her.

"I think I know how to use it..."

"Do the best you can." The woman was disappearing into the door. "I'll be back shortly!"

Without waiting for an answer, I took off across the green, sprinting past the booths and crossing the street to the front door of the hotel.

I burst through the glass doors into the quaint lobby, surprising both Maryann, the innkeeper, who was setting the tables in the dining room for tomorrow's breakfast, and Beth Collins, who had just started up the stairs.

"Beth!" I said. She turned around, startled.

"I hate to bother you, but can I talk to you for a minute?"

Her mouth turned down into a frown. "I'm a little short on time," she said.

"It'll only be a minute," I said, then turned to the innkeeper. "Is there somewhere private we can go to talk?"

"My husband's studio is right next door, across the court-yard," she said. "You can go in there; it should still be open."

"Why should I go with you?" Beth said.

"You used to go by Bethany, didn't you?" I asked.

She blinked. "How do you..." Her eyes darted to Maryann. "All right," she said, and followed me through the door at the end of the kitchen and through the dark courtyard to the door marked STUDIO.

The inside was small and dark and smelled like turpentine. I fumbled for a light switch; a single bulb lit up in the middle of the room, which was lined with paintings of farm animals. A large brown cow glared at me over Beth's shoulder. "What do you know?" she demanded.

"I know your name was originally Bethany Jackson," I said, ignoring the cow, "and that you ran a brewery in Houston with Felix Gustafson."

She blinked quickly. "That was a long time ago," she said. "And why do you care?"

"Someone dropped a bag of barley on Felix's head," I said. "Our sheriff arrested his brother. You knew them pretty well; do you think Simon would be capable of something like that?"

She paled, and her hand went to the beer bottle charm on her necklace. "They arrested Simon? Why?"

"I think the theory is Simon wanted to sign with your company and Felix didn't. So Simon decided to get his brother out of the way."

"No," she said, shaking her head. "I can't imagine he'd do something like that." A slender gold band with a big diamond twinkled on the fourth finger of her hand as she fingered the bottle charm nervously; next to it, a sold gold band gleamed.

"What happened between you and Felix?" I asked gently.

"It was a long time ago," she said in a bitter voice. "I try to forget."

"Tell me," I told her. "Please. It might help."

She sighed. "We were young and in love, and stupid enough to think that starting a business together was a good idea. It lasted about a year before it all blew up."

"The business? Or the relationship?"

"Both," she said. "He's just... he was, I mean... I still can't believe he's gone." Her eyes welled with tears, and she turned away.

"I'm so sorry." I touched her shoulder; she didn't move away. "Just because you weren't with him anymore doesn't mean you don't still care about him. He was a big part of your life."

"He was," she choked out, shoulders shaking. "If we hadn't started that stupid business, then maybe we'd still be together."

"You really loved him."

"I did," she told me in a voice filled with regret.

"Did he give you that necklace?" I asked, pointing to the gleaming bottle on a chain.

She looked down and touched the glass. "Yes. I don't know why I still wear it; I just got used to having it on, and it's part of my profession, so..."

"Things didn't work out between you, though."

"No." She shook her head, a sharp, decisive movement. "I loved him. But I couldn't live with him. So I left."

"What happened, if you don't mind my asking?"

She let out a ragged breath. "He was always chasing something. We had to have the best ingredients, the most unusual beer... he was just looking for the magic potion. The Holy Grail of beer, so to speak. And he would never stop chasing it."

"Hard to run a business like that."

She snorted. "You're telling me. He hated publicity and marketing, too. Said it felt 'false,' and that the beer should sell itself." Her words were laced with bitterness. "I mean, I'm sorry, but if you can't get your magic brew into stores, nobody's going to be able to buy it."

"And it was the same thing with Sweetwater, wasn't it?"

She nodded, face still turned away from me. "Simon got in touch with me about a month ago. Said they were in a different place now, and he and Felix would love the opportunity. Stupid me... I should have known better."

"Felix didn't want to join, did he?"

"Of course not," she said, an undertone of contempt in her voice. "Still chasing his utopian dream. Just like he did with Becca." Her voice turned flat. "I was a fool."

"Becca?"

"Becca was the brewer's assistant we hired. It took about a month before he was having it off with her." She let out a quick burst of sharp laughter. "Behind the fermentation tanks. So romantic, right? Anyway," she continued without prompting, "he told me that he'd spent the loan I'd managed to sweet-talk the bank into giving us to do some promotional work on a new, totally copper fermentation tank from Holland. They'd already shipped it, so he couldn't cancel the order. I ended up canceling all the advertising I'd set up, since I couldn't pay them, and the next month Felix moved in with Becca."

"That's awful," I said.

"Yeah. Apparently she really 'got' his vision. Supported him in ways I couldn't. So the business went under. It was registered in my name so it could be a woman-owned business, and I ended up with all the debt... and I found out after the fact that he was making thousands of dollars of personal purchases from the company account. I ended up filing for bankruptcy, and he just walked away."

"With another woman, no less."

"Oh, that didn't last. She must have gotten fed up with having to pay all the rent."

"Sounds like a pattern."

"You think?" she said bitterly, turning to look at me; her face was red, and her jaw set. "Sorry; I'm still sore about it. And now, even though he's gone, he's managed to saddle his brother with the same issue; I know Simon was struggling to pay the bills, but Felix wouldn't do a thing to help him. I wouldn't be surprised if he fouled his own beer just to scotch the deal... although I don't think he'd ever be able to bring himself to make something he did look bad."

From what I knew of what Nick had bought at the feed store, I had to agree with her assessment. "He sounds like he was a very selfish man."

"He was," she said. "Brilliant, charming, tremendous fun to be with... and selfish to the core. The only good thing about this whole mess is that that poor girl won't go through what I went through."

"What poor girl?"

"Teena, I think her name is? Max Pfeiffer told me all about her."

"Right. I heard you were talking with Max; are you thinking of signing his brewery?"

"We're talking about it. If he can get a better brewer and some marketing in place, maybe... he's trying to get someone to take over the brew room for him. I told him to get in touch with me when he's got things put together."

"So he's got to remake the business," I said.

"He was interviewing some local brewers last week... I think one of the assistant brewers at Sweetwater was one of them. But don't tell them I told you that; I probably should have kept that quiet."

"Apparently the assistant brewer skipped town," I said.

She looked startled. "When? Max didn't say anything about that."

"Maybe he's secretly working for Pfeiffer?" I suggested.

"Maybe," she said. "This whole thing has kind of been a soap opera, hasn't it?"

"It has," I agreed, and once again took in her newly dark and conservative hair, her business attire. "You kind of remade yourself after the Swamp Thang debacle, didn't you?"

She nodded. "I wanted to leave all of that—the bankruptcy, the failed relationship, the ruined business—behind me. The president of Brewlific took me on after I begged him."

"And you got married somewhere along the line, too," I commented, indicating the rings on her hand.

"I did," she said, and smiled for the first time. "Cameron is the love of my life. Solid, steady, and always, always in my corner. We're hoping to adopt a baby soon."

She did look like she was happily in love, despite her remaining bitterness toward Felix. Was she still angry enough to have killed him? I wondered. "Good for you," I said aloud. "It sounds like things are finally coming together for you."

"I've worked long and hard to prove myself, and it's starting to pay off. They recently promoted me to sales manager of the southwestern United States."

"Congratulations. I'll bet a lot of people are lining up to talk to you now."

"They are," she said, and a shadow of regret passed over her pretty face. "I was hoping to give Simon the opportunity, but with Felix gone..."

"I'd think that would make things easier," I pointed out.

She looked at me with sadness in her eyes. "You'd think

that, wouldn't you? But the thing is, for all his talk, he really did have a way with brewing. I don't know if Simon has access to his recipes; even if he did, he's always been on the business side of things, not the production end." Her voice changed from soft and regretful to firm and businesslike. "Plus, I did some research; Sweetwater's pretty leveraged. It's a risk. And harder now that Simon's been arrested," she added. "With both partners out of the picture, who's going to run the business?"

"That's why I want to find out what happened to Felix," I said. "Simon's already lost so much. If you're right, and he isn't responsible for what happened to his brother, it would be awful for him to lose everything and go to jail while the real culprit is walking free."

"I see your point," she said, then gave me a direct look from her brown eyes. "I've only been in town for a few days, so I have no idea who else Felix might have made mad enough to drop a sack of barley on his head." Then she gave a short, hard laugh that told me just how much he'd hurt her. "But knowing Felix, I'll bet there's more than a few candidates."

I HAD plenty to think about as I left the inn a few minutes later and walked back across the street to the bustling Oktoberfest. The Buttercup High School band had taken the stage and was playing a marching-band interpretation of "Edelweiss", and the smell of roasting meat, candied nuts, and kettle corn filled the air.

Even though Simon wasn't present at the Sweetwater booth, a crowd had gathered, and the young workers behind the table were busy filling mugs. I could hear the excited conversation as I walked by. "Rooster arrested him," a rancher I recognized was telling a friend. "Apparently he got fed up with his big-shot brother and put an end to things."

"I heard it was over a woman," the man he was talking to said. "I heard Simon was after one of Felix's ex-girlfriends."

"They were quite a pair, all right," someone else said. "I guess the brewery'll be back up for sale before you know it."

My heart twinged as I returned to the booth to relieve Teena of duty. She'd just told me how much she'd sold and headed off to the Sweetwater booth when Molly and Alfie Kramer strolled up.

"Hey, you!" Molly said, pulling me into a hug. I hugged her back, glad to see my friend.

"I've been caught up in school stuff and things have been busy at the the ranch, but I've been meaning to invite you over to coffee."

"That would be great," I said.

"Shame about what happened at the brewery. I hear Nick Schmidt wanted to work there, but his dad said he couldn't. Probably a good thing after all."

"He wanted to work there?" I asked.

"I think he's got a thing for Teena... Brittany told me that's why A&M didn't work out. He's obsessed with her."

"I didn't know that," I said, but I was thinking of the way he'd watched Teena the other day. Was there more to that than I knew?

"Nick's dad wants him to stop mooning over Teena, insisted he go to work for Ed. Thought hard physical labor would help him get over it and maybe appreciate school more."

"There's something to be said for that, I suppose," I replied. "He seems to be doing good work; I didn't know he was so into Teena, though."

"It's kind of creepy," she said. "Brittany told me he was outside Teena's house one night; her dad had to tell him to leave."

"Really?" I asked.

"He's got it bad. But you can't tell anyone I told you! Brittany told me in confidence."

"Got it," I said, but I was feeling uneasy.

"Nick was furious when he found out Teena and Felix had something going on," Molly said. "If you ask me, Felix was a bit old for her, really... I'm sad about what happened to him, of course, but maybe for Teena it's for the best. I think she may have been postponing school to hang out here because of him," Molly said.

"Wait," I said. "How do you know Nick was furious over Teena?"

"I found him shootin' skeet and swearin' up a storm out on the lower pasture," Alfie said; he'd been listening quietly as we spoke. "The Schmidts' property is right next to ours. I went out to find out what was goin' on, and Nick was in a right state."

"When was this?"

"The first day of Oktoberfest," Molly said. "Alfie came back to the ranch because some of the cattle weren't doing well."

"Nick was at my place earlier that day; the little Ulrich house almost fell down on top of him. Do you think that might be what it was?"

"No," Alfie said. He glanced around. "Just between us, he'd gone to try and talk to Teena, but Felix got to her place at the same time he did. Told him he was a little boy and needed to leave Teena to a real man."

"Ouch," I said, wincing. "I'm liking Felix less the more I find out about him."

"What else do you know?" Molly asked, eyes bright with curiosity.

"He's had a checkered romantic past, that's for sure. In business, too."

"Really?"

"I'll tell you about it if you guys come to dinner soon," I said. "But what's going on with the cattle?"

"Half of 'em came down lame," he said.

"Did you talk to Tobias?"

"I called him right away. He's been out twice. He isn't quite sure what's goin' on; he's been running some tests, though."

"I don't think you're the only one having that problem," I said. "I went out on a call with him the other day and it was the same thing, and Lotte at Heinrich Feed told me she's had a lot of ranchers with similar problems. She said something about a virus going around..."

"How are your livestock?" he asked.

"So far so good," I said. "My squash and cucumbers are dead, I had a bit of a raccoon issue in the chicken coop, and I found a kitten in my chimney, but so far everyone else is okay."

"You've had an exciting week!" Molly said. "And tell me more about the kitten? Are you keeping her?"

I had opened my mouth to answer when a scream pierced the Buttercup Band's oompah music. I jerked around to find the source; it was a coming from the direction of the Sweetwater booth.

I turned and sprinted over to the booth, hoping that Teena was okay, only to find her staring in horror at a barrel.

"What is it?" I asked as Molly and Alfie trotted up behind me.

"It's... it's a hand," the girl gasped.

17

"*W*hat happened?" I asked in a calm voice, catching the young woman's arm. Teena looked like she might faint again.

"Tracy here was trying to tap another barrel. But the beer wouldn't come out, so we opened it to see what was wrong, and..."

I followed the beam of the flashlight to the barrel and sucked in my breath. I could see more than a hand now; unless I was mistaken, the body in the barrel belonged to Sweetwater's assistant brewer, Billy Brindle.

"Someone needs to call the sheriff," I said quietly, and pulled out my phone.

IT WAS HALF an hour before Rooster bellied up to the booth, smelling like beer (not the Sweetwater variety) and looking extremely put out. The deputies in charge had cordoned off the area, and there was some quiet discussion of what to do next, but a grim pall had fallen over the whole festival. The band had taken a break and was playing again, but their usually perky music sounded more like a dirge.. Despite the bright blue-and-white buntings, the strings of lights, the music and the delicious smells wafting through the square, the spell had been broken, and there was a sense of hushed worry and fear among the scattering crowd.

"All right," Rooster said, hitching up his polyester pants, which looked like they were starting to get a little tight under his burgeoning beer belly. At least he'd dressed in uniform, I told myself. "Who found him?"

"We did," Teena told him, and she explained what had happened.

Rooster grabbed the flashlight from his belt and shone it into the barrel. "Do we know who the poor fella is?"

"I think it's Billy Brindle, the assistant brewer," I said.

He turned and flashed the light into my face. "What are you doin' here?"

"I heard a scream. I came to make sure everyone was okay."

"Looks like you got here a little late," he remarked, then let out a heavy sigh. "I guess I gotta get forensics back out here, since I don't see how he'd manage to get himself in a barrel."

He was right about that, I thought. As he dialed, I scanned the faces of the folks standing around. Most of them were young, and they looked scared. I'd entertained thoughts of Adriana or Beth/Bethany killing Felix to settle a romantic score, but this new discovery quashed that line of inquiry. I glanced around again; Nick was standing in the shadows behind the booth, eyes fixed on Teena, propped up on crutches.

The boy in the barrel had liked Teena. Too much, and

way too insistently. A chill ran through me as I looked at Nick, whose face was shrouded in shadow.

Was he just a young man misunderstood by his father and trying to make his way in the world?

Or was he an obsessive stalker who was willing to get rid of any obstacle between him and the object of his affection?

MOLLY STOPPED BACK by the farm's booth just as I finished boxing up the last of the soaps. "Hey," I said.

"Hey," she replied. "You need help packing up?"

"No," I said, glancing around, "but I wanted to ask you a few questions about Nick Schmidt."

She blinked at me. "Why?"

"You know how he likes Teena?" I asked.

She nodded.

"Well, I think he was so jealous of Felix that he put sulfur in the beer Felix tapped at the Oktoberfest opening to make it go off. I didn't think Nick could be responsible for what happened to Felix—someone cut the cable to drop the barley—but the young man in that barrel also had a crush on Teena, and I saw him hitting on her with him the other day at the brewery."

"You don't think... you think Nick's a killer? But what about his leg?"

"Maybe he killed Billy before he broke his leg," I suggested. "When did Billy go missing?"

"Yesterday," Molly said.

"And when did Nick break his leg?"

"This morning," she told me.

"So we can't rule him out," I said. Then, with horror, I realized that in both the case of the accidents to the construction sites and Felix's murder, cables had been cut. And I'd seen Nick at the brewery just before Felix was killed.

Even if he had murdered Felix, though, why would Nick cut the cables on a building he was working in?

"But he's over at your house working on the renovation, and you're there alone with him!" she said, echoing my own thoughts.

"I'm not interested in a romantic relationship with Teena," I pointed out, trying to hide my uneasiness.

"No," she said. "But if he thinks you're onto him..."

"We still don't know if he's responsible for any of this," I reminded her. "It's just a theory."

"Be careful," she said. "Can you postpone the renovation till you know?"

"I don't think so," I said. "If Ed gets that Buttercup Bank job, I need him to finish the house up before he starts on that. Otherwise I have no way of getting it done before the antique fair. And I don't want those appliances I bought just sitting around."

"I see what you mean," she said. "Still..." She gave me a warning look. "Be careful."

CHUCK WAS WAITING at the front door for me, the kitten batting at his tail, when I got home about an hour later. "How are you guys?" I asked, bending down to pet them both. "I'll bet you're hungry," I told the rumbling kitten. "Let me just get the cold stuff put up and then I'll feed you, okay?"

As I put the few remaining flans back into the fridge, the two animals galloped around the kitchen together, Chuck almost knocking me over as he raced across the floor. I was happy to see him so active; he'd been slowing down lately, and although I hadn't said anything to Tobias about it yet, it had been worrying me.

I fixed their food dishes and put them down on the floor —the new arrival was becoming good at feeding herself— and then unloaded the rest of my wares from the truck, still thinking about what had happened that night.

I hadn't seen Adriana at the Oktoberfest festival, but that didn't mean she hadn't been there. Besides, whoever had killed Billy had likely done it before the barrel ever left the brewery. And Adriana's beef had been with Felix and Simon, not Billy. At the thought of Simon, I wondered: Did finding another body while Simon was in jail help let him off the hook?

Probably not, I decided. Billy had disappeared before Simon was arrested. Even though it would be horrible business sense to hide your dead assistant brewer in a barrel from your own brewery, I knew Rooster wouldn't quickly give up on an easy suspect. Besides, it was likely that Billy had died before Simon was arrested... and I at least knew of a potential motive, since Beth had told me Billy had probably interviewed with Max Pfeiffer for a job as head brewer. Was Simon so obsessed with his business that he was willing to kill both his brother and Billy to keep them from damaging it? After all, the assistant brewer had access to all of Felix's recipes. I was sure that was some of the appeal for Max; if they could replicate Sweetwater's brews and then market themselves to Brewlific, Max would have a good chance of putting Sweetwater out of business.

Somehow, I decided, I needed to talk to Max Pfeiffer and find out if he had indeed interviewed Billy... and what they had decided in terms of his future. Or theoretical future, I thought with a pang. Although I hadn't liked Billy when I met him, it upset me that someone young had died. What had happened to him? I wondered uneasily. And was Nick really responsible?

And if so, how had he managed to get into the brewery to kill him and put him in a barrel?

I finished unpacking the truck, but was still restless. Chuck and the kitten were busy tumbling around the kitchen again, now happily fed, but my stomach was rumbling; with everything that had happened, I hadn't had a chance to grab something to eat.

But first I had to take care of the livestock and check on my crops. Chores on a farm, unfortunately, wait for no woman.

Everyone was waiting for me, anxious to be milked, when I stepped outside into the cool, star-studded evening. A breeze had come up from the north, ahead of a line of clouds that looked like it might promise rain again. Although we'd had too much rain earlier in the summer, we'd gone a week or so without much to speak of, so I'd be thankful for it now. The cool, green-smelling breeze felt good against my skin; despite the work still waiting for me, I paused to let it blow the hair back from my face, and took a long, deep breath. Then I opened my eyes and took in the peaceful, starlit scene. A trickle of water murmured from Dewberry Creek, and the breeze ruffled the sycamore trees, bringing me a whiff of their honey-scented leaves. The oaks and pecans, I knew, were heavy with nuts; it was going to be a mast year, with plenty for both the squirrels and me. There would be pecan pie, and dewberry cobbler from the berries I had picked that spring, and pear butter on toast from the two trees I'd put in when I moved to the farm; I'd harvested almost a bushel in August, and had made my first batch of pear butter just a few weeks ago. It was for moments like this that I'd moved to Buttercup, and even with everything else going on, I didn't want to forget to appreciate them.

After another deep, sycamore-scented breath, I headed to the barn, resolved not to let the upsetting events of the day throw me completely off balance. I had led Blossom to the milking parlor and was about to start when I realized I'd used the last of the feed that morning; I had nothing to keep her busy while I worked.

"Sorry about that, Blossom," I said, touching her soft nose, then headed out to the truck to lug one of the bags of feed in. I plopped it on the floor and eyed it suspiciously. Should I use it?

I pulled out my phone and called Tobias, but the call went to voice mail. "Hey, sweetheart. I just bought some cattle feed at Heinrich's Feed today; I'm not sure if I should use it or not. Can you give me a call back?"

When I hung up, I debated for a moment. Tobias seemed to think there might be some issue with the feed, and this bag looked different from the others. Was it possible that contaminated feed was the problem? And was what I'd bought today the same feed the others had used? Blossom gave me an impatient moo and stamped her feet, and I decided to risk it; it was only a little bit, and if there was a problem with the feed, the store would have pulled it, right?

I cut the top of the bag with the pocket knife I kept handy and scooped some of it out for Blossom, who set to gratefully. The milking went smoothly—Hot Lips was the main culprit when it came to kicking, and she was settling down more every day—and I had led Gidget into the stall and was about to finish up when there was a ruckus from the chicken coop. Russell was crowing louder than I'd ever heard him.

"Sorry, girl... I'll be right back," I said, patting Gidget and hurrying to the door of the barn, just in time to see a gray tabby streaking away from the chicken coop, Russell crowing indignantly and ruffling his feathers.

As I watched her disappear through the fence and slip like a shadow into a stand of wild plums, I wondered what to do about her... and if there were any other kittens hidden somewhere near the farm.

I returned to milk Gidget, who was giving me an accusing look from her golden eyes, and got everyone settled for the night before taking the milk into the kitchen and heading out to the coop, my eyes straying to the dark mass I knew to be a thicket of plums.

She was still here, it seemed. And I still had to figure out what to do about her.

I HAD JUST FINISHED PROCESSING the goats' milk and was in the middle of making another batch of mozzarella cheese with the cows' milk when a truck bumped up the driveway, headlights bouncing. Chuck let out a low growl and headed to the door, barking, the kitten trailing in his wake. The headlights were too low to the ground to be Tobias's. Who was visiting me after dark, unannounced?

Adrenaline pulsed in me, and I reached for the baseball bat Tobias had insisted I keep in the umbrella stand by the front door, just in case.

The car screeched to a stop, and I recognized it as Teena's Honda Civic.

I relaxed and slid the bat back into the umbrella stand,

then opened the door to greet her, Chuck and the kitten at my feet.

"What's up?" I asked. "Are you okay?"

"I'm fine," she said. "I just... I feel like I need to talk to you."

"About what?" I asked.

"That's the thing," she said, scraping her long hair back out of her face with an agitated gesture. "I just don't know."

"Well, come on in and we'll figure it out," I said.

18

I led her into the kitchen. As she sat down at the big pine farm table, she was mobbed by the animal contingent of the house. "Who are these cuties?" she asked as Chuck jumped up on her and the kitten looked up and meowed.

"This is Chuck," I said, gesturing to the overexcited poodle, who was loving the head scratches Teena was doling out, "and the kitten is a new arrival. We found her in the chimney, and Chuck seems to have adopted her."

"She's adorable!" Teena cooed, reaching down to pick up the little gray fluff ball, who started purring immediately.

I smiled as the kitten half-closed her eyes in apparent ecstasy. "Do you want a glass of iced tea?" I offered. "Or a ginger beer?"

"I'll take a ginger beer," she said as she followed me into the kitchen, the kitten in her arms and Chuck at her heels. I popped the caps off two bottles and handed one to her before taking a swig out of the second.

"I was just going to process this milk," I told her. "Maybe

when I'm done, we can go down to the Ulrich house and you can see what you think?"

"We can, but that's not why I'm here," she said, sitting down and stroking the kitten. "Whatever I'm here for has to do with something else. Maybe Felix." Her eyes welled with tears again, and as she said Felix's name, a strong, sharp smell of lavender filled my nostrils.

"Do you smell that?" I asked.

"Your grandmother's here, isn't she?" Teena asked with a dreamy smile. She set the kitten down to play and looked around my cozy kitchen. "I used to come here from time to time when I was small. I haven't been here since your grandmother passed, but her presence is still strong." Her eyes were unfocused. "She's glad you're here."

"I feel that too," I said.

"She wants to help," Teena said. "She told me to check by the cistern."

"By the cistern? What's by the cistern?"

Teena snapped back into focus. "I don't know. It's just what she said."

"We'll look when I'm done," I said, feeling goose bumps spring up on my arms. I rubbed them down, then gave the curds on the stove a stir with a wooden spoon and checked the thermometer. "In the meantime, I wanted to ask you about Nick."

She blinked. "Nick Schmidt? What about him?"

"Has he ever asked you out or anything?"

Teena's cheeks turned a shade of pink. "Yeah," she told me. "He's kind of had a thing for me for a while. I'm just not interested, but he still keep trying."

"That's got to be frustrating," I said. "How has he kept trying?"

"He's always... well, hanging around. Watching me. And

when he found out Felix and I were seeing each other..." She shivered, and her eyes grew big. "Wait. He got upset with one of the guys at the brewery the other day, too. I was talking to him at the brewery, laughing about how crazy Felix was about people touching the Dubbel Trouble barrels, and Nick... well, Jack touched me on the shoulder, and Nick came up and told him he was out of line." She swallowed. "He threatened to beat him up, but Jack backed away and told him to chill."

"Wow," I said. I hadn't seen any of that behavior from Nick. "That's got to be uncomfortable."

"It is," she said. "I felt him watching me at the brewery the other day, and I'm pretty sure I've seen him drive by my house a few times lately. Do you think maybe..."

"Maybe what?" I asked, hoping she wasn't coming to the same conclusion I was.

"Do you think Nick killed Felix and Billy?" she asked in a small voice.

"I don't know," I said. I knew he'd been angry enough to put sulfur in Felix's beer... but was he capable of murder? My heart hurt at the thought of someone so young being driven to such an awful act. Then again, his behavior regarding Teena had been far from acceptable, from what she had told me. Bordering on stalking. "What do you think?" I asked in a level voice.

She closed her eyes. "He's angry. But there's someone else who's angry, too. I get red and white."

"Red and white," I said. "Like someone at the Red & White store?"

"I don't know," she said. "That's all that's coming for now." Again, that strong whiff of lavender. "It's about history," she said, eyes wide open. "Making sure it doesn't repeat itself."

"That's what you said when you fainted at the brewery," I said.

"It's what keeps coming back," she said.

"Right. So we've got the Red & White and making sure history doesn't repeat itself," I said, trying to figure out what that meant. "The only history I can think of is the names Max Pfeiffer wants to keep. What was his family's brewery called?"

"The Bluff Springs Brewery," she said. "It started in a historic site that's now a park; he wanted to put it there, but the property belongs to the State of Texas now."

I gave the milk a stir and checked the temperature, then grabbed my laptop from the counter. "Bluff Springs Brewery?"

"I think that's what it was called," she said. I typed in the name.

"Found it," I said. "It was started in the late 1840s by Heinrich Pfeiffer. He was a mason from Germany; he managed to build the first brewery in Texas that kept things cool enough to make the first lager."

"How did he do that?" she asked.

"Evidently he built some kind of tunnel system that kept the temperature down even in hot weather," I said, reading. "He had *'Frisch Auf'* parties, with dances and drinking, that the whole community came to; Bluff Springs Beer was a huge success for a while there."

"That's the slogan Max Pfeiffer was upset about," Teena said. "*Frisch Auf.*"

"Right," I said.

"What happened to the brewery?"

"Apparently a rival brewer set up shop nearby and took over half their sales. They were about to go bankrupt when Heinrich died."

"How?" Teena asked.

I looked up at her. "Crushed by a load of stones."

"Just like Felix," she whispered.

"It was ruled an accident, but there was an inquest," I said, reading on. "The other brewery started brewing lager and Bluff Springs Beer faded away."

"History repeating itself..." Teena said.

I got up and checked on the milk, which was coming along. "Max Pfeiffer was angry at Simon and Felix for using some of his family's brewery's trademarks, even though they weren't officially trademarks," I said. "And apparently Max interviewed Billy for a job this week."

"Wait a moment," Teena said. "Are you thinking Max Pfeiffer killed Felix and Billy out of some kind of retribution? It doesn't make sense if he wanted to hire Billy. Why kill the person who's supposed to bring the recipes to your company?"

"Maybe Billy refused?" I suggested. Honestly, based on what she'd told me, Nick seemed like a more likely candidate. But as far as I knew, the only history I could connect the current crimes with involved the Bluff Springs Brewery. And I still couldn't figure out what any of it had to do with the Red & White.

"I'm going to go talk with Max Pfeiffer tomorrow," I said, giving the milk a stir; it was close to coming to temperature.

"About what?" Teena asked.

I thought about it for a moment. "I'll tell him I'm considering growing hops, and see if he's interested in buying any."

"That sounds like a plan," she said. "But be careful. Do you want me to come with you?"

"You work for his archenemy," I said. "Probably not."

"True," she said. "But I don't like you going there alone. You know, in case."

"I'll figure something out," I said. We hung out in the kitchen for a few more minutes until the milk came to temperature. Then I turned down the stove and put a lid on the pot. "This is finally done. Let's go check out the cistern."

"Got it," she said. I grabbed a flashlight and headed out the kitchen door, leaving Chuck and the kitten inside.

The breeze had picked up since I was last outside. "Do you think we'll get some rain?" Teena asked as we walked to the back gate.

"I hope so," I said.

"I heard you lost a lot of your pumpkins and cucumbers," she said. "Sorry to hear that; I know that's a lot of work."

"The joys of farming," I quipped. "Hey... do you know what went wrong with the barley deal Adriana made with the brewery?"

"Oh, that," she said, rolling her eyes. "That's been just a nightmare. They were all excited about the agreement, but you know how we had a wet spring?"

"I remember it well," I said. The rain—both too much and too little—this year had been part of my problem.

"Well, barley's a cool-season crop here. And apparently, under the right conditions, it can be infected with some kind of fungus. Felix told me it had something to do with something called Saint Elmo's Fire back in the Middle Ages. Made people go crazy, was mixed up with witch burnings, I think he said."

"I thought Saint Elmo's Fire was a weather event."

"Maybe I got the name wrong," she said as we closed the gate behind us and headed down the path to the old cistern, "but it was something like that. Anyway, he couldn't use the barley—said it would make everybody sick—but Adriana didn't believe him. She threatened a lawsuit, but finally backed off."

"So some bad blood there."

"For sure," Teena agreed. "I heard she finally sold it, though, so maybe he was wrong."

"Do you think maybe he was just trying not to spend the money?"

"Felix wasn't like that," Teena said. "Simon was always after him to keep ingredient cost lower, but Felix always refused to compromise on quality."

I didn't tell Teena that Felix and Adriana had had a relationship prior to (and perhaps during) their courtship—after all, it would just cause more pain—but I filed what she told me away.

As I flashed the light toward the cistern, something gray streaked past us. "What was that?" Teena asked.

"Mother cat, I think."

"Does she have any other kittens?" Teena asked.

"I don't know," I said. "Chuck and I kind of searched the perimeter, but we didn't find anything. We think she was in the smokehouse, and a raccoon came in and tried to steal her babies. Our best guess is that she put this one into the chimney to keep her safe, but we have no idea if there are any others."

"Where's the cistern?" she asked.

"Over here," I said, hitching a left at the side path leading to the cistern. "We found it not long ago; it must have been built a hundred years ago. It was all grown over."

When we got there, the lid was ajar.

"Is it always like this?"

"No," I said. "That's dangerous." As I went to push it, there was a small mewling sound from deep inside. I aimed the flashlight down. Roots lined the dark pit; and at the bottom, clinging to a branch just above the water, was another kitten.

"This is what she was talking about, then," Teena breathed. "What do we do?"

"She's too far down to reach," I said.

"How deep is it?"

"I don't know," I said. "Stay here; I've got a rope emergency ladder in the barn." I'd kept it at my old condo in Houston in case I needed to make a second-floor escape.

"What are you going to attach the ladder to?" she asked.

"That tree," I said, pointing to a pecan tree growing about ten feet away from the cistern. "I'll need some rope to tie it, though."

"I hope you're good with knots," Teena said as I hurried back up the path to the barn.

The ladder was in the loft where I remembered leaving it, thankfully—I should probably move it to the house anyway, I reflected—and I grabbed the coil of rope I kept on a hook by the door before hurrying back down to the cistern, the rope looped over my shoulder and the ladder clutched under my arm.

"I hope this is long enough," I said as I dropped the ladder next to the cistern and took the rope to the tree. I looped it around and tied it, then headed back to the ladder.

"How does this work?" Teena asked.

"We unfold it like this," I said, undoing the strap that kept it together, "and then lower it gently into the cistern to see how far it goes. Can you hold the end and I'll drop it down slowly?"

"Got it," she said, and grabbed the top hooks as I began feeding the ladder down the cistern. When it was fully extended, it was still five feet from the kitten. Teena looked up at me, her face reflected in the glow from the water below. "Now what?"

"We'll have to use the rope to extend it," I said. I

measured out about five extra feet on the rope and tied it to the top rung of the ladder.

"I hope you're good with knots," Teena repeated.

"Thanks for the encouraging words," I said as I tied the best knot I could and lowered the ladder down.

"What do I do if you fall in?"

"Try to fish me out? And call for help if you have to," I suggested.

"Okay," she said, not sounding too confident about things. "Are you sure this is a good idea?"

"No," I told her straight out. "But I don't have any other ideas, so this is the one we're going with."

As Teena watched, I pushed the lid the rest of the way over and lay down on my stomach, inching myself feet-first until my toe hit the top rung of the ladder. I scooted down until both feet were on the top rung and took a deep breath. "Here goes nothing," I said, and put my whole weight on the top rung, holding onto the rope for balance. I swung back and forth a few times, praying the rope would hold, while Teena made anxious noises from somewhere above me, shining the light right in my eyes. I looked down and away. Then I took a step down, and another, my eyes fixed on the kitten, who appeared to be an orange tabby and was (thankfully) still clinging to the root. The end of the ladder dangled two feet above the kitten; I was going to have to hold onto the ladder and reach down to scoop him or her up.

"Hang in there, sweetheart," I murmured, as much to myself as to the kitten, as I took another step down. The air was cold and dank and earthy smelling, and the wall of the cistern was slimy. Who had built it? And had anyone else fallen down it? I shivered and put the thought out of my head; even though my grandparents had owned the farm for as long as I remembered, there was still a lot I didn't know about it.

After what seemed like an hour, I reached the last rung. The kitten was just a few feet beneath me, looking up at me with green eyes that matched his or her sister's. "I've got you," I said gently, and squatted down on the last rung to grab the little creature. I had just closed my hand around the kitten's thin little body when the ladder gave way, dropping both me and the kitten into the cold, dark water.

19

*I*t felt like being dunked in a bucket of ice water. I instinctively held the kitten up over my head, keeping it above water, but I inhaled what seemed like a gallon of water and came up spluttering.

"Lucy!" Teena called from far above me. "Are you okay?"

"I'm fine for now," I called back, "and so is the kitten, but we can't stay here for long."

"The knot must have come loose. What do I do?" she asked, sounding panicky.

"Call Tobias, for starters," I said. "Is the rope long enough to go all the way down to me?" I thought so, but I hadn't actually measured it.

"Are you going to climb it?" she asked.

Rope-climbing had been my absolute nemesis in elementary school gym class, but I could only hope that the work on the farm had increased my upper body strength. Or, failing that, that adrenaline would do the trick.

"I'm going to try," I said. "How are you with knots?"

"Hopefully better than you," she said. The flashlight disappeared, and I busied myself treading water using two feet and one hand; the other hand was holding the limp kitten above me and out of the water. I paddled to the side until I found a tree root I could hold onto, then moved the kitten to my shoulder and grabbed the slimy root.

I could hear her voice above me; hopefully she'd gotten hold of Tobias. A minute or two later, the light came back. "I untied it and retied it to the tree to make it as long as possible," she called down. "Let's hope it reaches!" As she spoke, the rope slithered down the side of the cistern. She lowered it until it came to an end... about eighteen inches out of my reach.

"It's not quite long enough," I said.

"Oh, no. What do we do now?"

"Hang on," I said. "I might be able to reach it. Let me try."

I took a deep breath and submerged myself completely, using my feet to kick as hard as I could and launch me out of the water. It got me closer, but not close enough. I gasped for air, tasting clay and dankness in my mouth, and tried again.

Still nothing. The kitten mewled, frightened by the ruckus I'd created, and hunched up against the wall. So far this rescue attempt was not going well.

"Now what?" Teena asked.

"I'm thinking," I informed her.

"Is there more rope?"

"Not that I can think of," I said. "Wait. I've got sheets in the linen closet. Can you go grab one of those?"

"I don't want to leave you here!"

"It's okay," I said. "I can hold on, and even if I couldn't, I used to do swim team in high school. I can tread water for a few minutes."

"If you're sure..."

"I'm sure," I said. A moment later, the light vanished

again, leaving only a small circle dotted with stars above me and the faint mewl of a frightened kitten echoing in the dank cistern.

BY THE TIME she came back, I was starting to feel chilled, and the kitten was starting to tremble from the cold. I didn't know how long he or she had been down here, but I was afraid if we didn't get out soon, the poor thing's chances might be low.

The rope jerked back up the side of the cistern before slithering over the top and disappearing. "I'm doing the best knot I can," Teena announced, and a minute later, the rope came back down, a white sheet like a flag at the end of it. When it was fully extended, the bottom corner of the sheet was in the water, glowing white in the light of Teena's flashlight.

"Ready?" I called.

"Ready," she said. "I'll hold the rope just in case something goes wrong."

"Make sure you don't end up in here with me," I warned her. Then I retrieved the shivering kitten from the tree root and tucked him into the top of my shirt; his wet body was cold against my skin.

"Here goes nothing," I muttered, and grabbed the sheet, using my feet to brace me against the wall.

Thankfully, the knot held—at least the knot holding the sheet to the rope—and before long I was grasping the rough rope, moving slowly, hand-over hand, my feet walking up the wall.

My arms were screaming with pain, but I didn't let go. The starry circle at the top of the cistern grew closer and closer. I was just over halfway there when the kitten wriggled and slipped down my chest to my stomach.

I couldn't let go of the rope or I'd fall, so I tucked my elbows close to my body. "Don't move," I said, praying that this rescue attempt didn't end in me dropping the kitten ten feet from the top of the cistern.

The kitten slipped again, letting out a little mewl. "No," I breathed. At that moment, the scent of lavender, sharp and sweet, replaced the cold dankness of the cistern. I felt the kitten latch onto my shirt with its sharp little claws, and almost as if someone were guiding it, climb back up so that it was latched to the shirt just above my breastbone.

"Thank you," I murmured, and with new purpose, reached up and moved another foot toward the opening.

My arms and legs were on fire by the time I reached the top. "Grab the kitten," I begged Teena breathlessly. I didn't want to crush the poor thing trying to lever myself over the edge of the cistern.

Teena bent down and detached her from my shirt, then reached out to my hand with her free one. "Let me help you," she said, and with her warm hand, helped pull me over the edge of the cistern onto the good, dry earth.

"Thank you so much for your help," I told her when we'd gotten back to the house a few minute later. I'd wrapped the kitten in warm towels and offered him a little bit of the kitten food Tobias had left me; he ate a few bites and drank some water before snuggling into my chest. Both Chuck and the gray kitten were fascinated by the new arrival. When I let them sniff him, the gray kitten stretched out a small paw and rested it on the second

kitten's face. The orange tabby opened his green eyes—
exactly the same shade as the first kitten's—and started
purring.

"I think they recognize each other," Teena said.

"I think so too," I said. Chuck had lain down on the rug
by the stove. On impulse, I tucked the orange kitten in next
to him. He curled around him, and the gray kitten padded
over and snuggled into his other side. I tucked the warm
towel over them—I could hear the two kittens purring—and
stood back, smiling.

"You've got a whole little family here, don't you?" Teena
said, a soft smile on her young face.

"I'd been thinking about getting a cat. Now I've got two."

"Three, if you can catch their mama," she pointed out.

"True," I said. "I wonder if there are any more out there?"

Teena paused for a moment, looking as if she were
listening, then shook her head. "I think that's it."

"Well, then," I said. "All we need now is names."

"Smoky seems about right for the gray one," I said, "since
we found her in the chimney."

"How about Lucky for the orange one?'" Teena suggested
with a grin.

I laughed. "He certainly is."

≈

TOBIAS RACED to the farm as soon as I called him, and after
making sure I was generally unscathed, checked the new
kitten out. He proclaimed him not totally healthy, but not in
imminent danger, and after Teena left, we snuggled the
three animals together in the middle of my bed.

"Any luck on figuring out what's going on with the
cattle?" I asked as the kittens purred contentedly.

"I think it's ergotism," he said. "Remember those black flecks I noticed in the feed?"

"I do. What's ergotism?"

"Ergot is a fungus that gets into some grain in cool, wet conditions; that's what the black flecks were. Historically, infected grain has been used in bread, beer, and other things with less-than-terrific results. In people, it causes a condition they used to call it Saint Anthony's Fire in the Middle Ages. They think it may have been associated with some of the witch trials; it can cause hallucinations and other issues."

"Teena was talking about that just today!" I said, sitting up. "She called it St. Elmo's Fire, which I knew was wrong, and said something about Adriana's barley having some kind of fungus associated with it. Must have been because of the wet spring we had; we had a few late cold fronts, too, before the heat arrived. Anyway, that must be why Sweet-water didn't buy it."

"Good thing they didn't," Tobias said. "That could have been really bad. Do you know who she ended up selling it to?"

"No, but I've got a good guess," I said, thinking of Lotte at the feed store and all the cattle who had mysteriously been coming down sick.

"I didn't think that could be it, since it's not anything I've encountered in Texas before. But I did some research on the symptoms, and everything points to ergotism."

"I'll bet Adriana sold her barley as cattle feed," I said. "And the mill didn't know enough to turn it away."

"I'll know for sure if that's what it is shortly," Tobias said. "I sent a sample to be tested. But in the meantime, I'd stick to hay."

"I will," I said. "Will the cows recover?"

"If they're switched to uninfected feed, I hope so," he said.

"I'm glad you've got that figured out," I told him.

"Well, that's my theory, anyway. And what you told me about the barley Sweetwater refused makes me think I'm on the right track. Even if Adriana's grain wasn't the source, if hers was infected, there's a good chance someone else's was."

"With any luck, that's one mystery solved; and hopefully with no casualties, I said."

"Speaking of casualties," he said, raising an eyebrow at me, "next time you go down a cistern, could you have someone who isn't a teenager as backup?"

"She's very responsible. I had her leave you a message," I said. "And it all worked out okay. I was afraid if I left him down there much longer that he wouldn't make it."

"He might not have," Tobias acknowledged. "Hypothermia's dangerous"

"Well, all's well that ends well," I said. "At least as far as the kittens go. We just have to trap the mama. I've been leaving food out for her, and it's disappearing, but I'm not sure if it's the mama cat or the raccoon who's eating it."

"Just keep leaving it out," he said. "I know you think we've got all the kittens, but I'd rather wait a little bit anyway, just to be sure. Maybe she'll get used to you and be easier to trap."

"Maybe," I said. "Here's hoping." I petted the kittens' heads, amazed at how perfect the little creatures were, and grateful we'd managed to save both of them.

I just wished I could figure out the mystery of what had happened to Felix—and Billy.

~

AFTER FINISHING my chores the next day, I called Quinn.

"Are you up for a field trip?" I asked.

"What do you mean?"

"I want to talk to Max and ask about Billy and the head brewer job."

"So you're going to talk with a murder suspect, and you want me to come with you?"

I shrugged. "Strength in numbers? I'm not going to tell him he's a murder suspect. I'm just going to tell him... well, I don't know what I'm going to tell him, but I need to know what happened about the job."

"Sounds like a solid plan."

"I'll come up with something; and you'll be with me if I get into trouble. Tobias chided me for going down a cistern with only a teenager present to help me if something went wrong. You're not a teenager, so I should be okay."

"What? What cistern?"

"I'll tell you if you come with me. Will you?"

"I'm probably an idiot, but yes. Have you told Tobias you're going?"

"I plan to tell him when we're on our way."

"And I'll tell Peter." She sighed. "I do wish we had a gun."

"You're testing for a black belt soon. Besides, don't you still have some pepper spray?"

"I do!" she said brightly. "Thanks for reminding me. What time shall I expect you?"

"I'm on my way over, if you're free."

"I'll be here with bells on," she said.

20

The Pfeiffer brewery was a very different operation from Sweetwater. Instead of neatly manicured gardens and clean-looking buildings, Max Pfeiffer's brewery was a small collection of derelict buildings decorated liberally with discarded tires, rusted-out appliances, and the carcasses of two ancient pick-up trucks.

I pulled in next to an old Ford pick-up, which was the only vehicle not on blocks in the overgrown gravel lot, killed the engine, and turned to Quinn. "Got your pepper spray?"

"Right in my pocket," she said, patting the right leg of her pants. "Got your plan?"

"I think so," I said.

"That's encouraging."

"We'll be fine," I said. "How's the battery on your phone?" I asked.

"Eight-seven percent," she reported.

"Can you put it on record? In case we get something interesting?"

She shrugged. "Sure." She set up the phone to record and

tucked it into the front pocket of her blouse. Then we both took deep breaths and got out of the truck.

"What now?" she asked.

"I think the main part of the brewery looks like it's over there," I said, pointing to the large, barn-like structure behind a squat brick house and two sheds in various stages of deterioration. The big front doors were open, and although I couldn't see anyone, I could hear the humming of machinery from inside.

"Does he not have anyone working for him?" she asked. "Seems like a lot to run a brewery by yourself."

"Maybe that's why he was talking with Billy," I said. "Shall we?"

"Might as well get it over with," she said.

The smell of beer was strong as we walked into the barn. "Hello?" I called.

"Who's there?" The voice was gruff, and came from the back corner, behind several pallets of white cans with scarlet lettering labeled, simply, with no extra graphics, PFEIFFER DARK BEER. It reminded me of a generic label in a grocery store. No wonder Max was losing out to Sweetwater.

"Lucy Resnick and Quinn Sloane. We were on our way to LaGrange and decided to stop by," I lied.

"What do you want?" Max was a bit wobbly, it seemed; in his right hand was a blue can marked PFEIFFER LAGER. He took a swig as he stood there, and I got a sour whiff off him; he'd definitely been drinking. I looked around at the complicated system of tanks and pipes; it looked not nearly as clean as what I'd seen at Sweetwater, and there was a lot less of it, since Pfeiffer had a smaller concern, but that didn't make it any less dangerous.

"I heard you were talking with Beth Collins about

joining up with Brewlific," I said, cutting to the chase. His scalp gleamed under the long strands of gray hair, which appeared not to have been washed for a while. Nor had his John Deere T-shirt, it seemed; it was so dirty I could barely identify the logo. "Someone mentioned you interviewed Billy Brindle about joining up with the brewery. I'm sure you know what happened to him... I was wondering if he said anything about feeling under threat at Sweetwater?"

"That place was a racket," he said. "I wouldn't work there if you paid me."

I was pretty sure that's how employment worked generally—you got paid for working—but I just smiled at him and asked, "Why?"

"They're all about that marketing stuff. And they're greedy... taking what isn't theirs."

"I understand they took over some things from the brewery your family used to own."

"That's right," he said. "They didn't even ask. Just took it. Come in with all their fancy marketing things... they're not even from here. What right do they have to horn in on my turf?"

"I can see it would be upsetting. I was kind of surprised to see you at the brewery, actually. What made you decide to go?"

"Competitive market research," he said. "Plus, I wanted to meet Miz Collins, talk to her about going with a real local business, not some jumped-up big-city enterprise."

"How did it go?"

He looked down and to the left. "We're talkin'," he said.

"I'm sure your odds are much better now that Felix is gone and Simon's in jail," Quinn said. A small smile played around his mouth, but he said nothing. "It must have been a disappointment to lose Billy, though. He had all of Felix's recipes, I hear."

"He was a waste of time," Max said. His face reddened as he spoke. "Cocky millennial, if you ask me."

"So he said no," I said.

"He didn't see quality and history when he saw it!" Anger contorted Max's face. "My grandfather Helmut died for his craft. I won't see his legacy destroyed by some cocky young upstart. You know what happened to my great-grandfather, right?"

"What did happen?" I asked. "I read he died in some sort of accident?"

"One of his rivals dropped a ton of stone on him. And then they drove his poor widow out of business."

"That's awful," I said. "I'm so sorry."

"Well," he said, "you can see I wasn't going to let history repeat itself."

I wasn't sure exactly what that meant—no one, to my knowledge, had threatened to drop a bunch of rocks on Max —but "history repeats itself" was exactly what Teena had said when Felix died. I was beginning to believe Quinn and I had figured out who had killed Felix—and probably Billy. But how did that fit in with the Red & White?

"Billy sounds like he was a real jerk," I said. "What exactly did he say to you to make you so angry?"

"He said he'd rather drink horse piss than... well, I won't tell you what he said," he spluttered, and took another swig from the can in his hand. "And then he was goin' to talk to that woman who calls herself a reporter, down at the *Buttercup Zephyr*."

"That sounds horrible," I said. "What was he going to tell her?"

"That..." He looked away. "That I'd tried to hire him away,

of course. Anyway, it doesn't matter. Sweetwater is dead in the water, and I'm busy; I've got work to do, filling all these cans." He pointed to a pallet of red and white cans waiting to be filled.

Red & White. Red and white. The can next to Felix's dead body had been red and white.

I swallowed hard.

"It was kind of poetic justice," I said, "being able to drop that load of barley on Felix's head."

"It was," he said, puffing his chest out. "He got what he deserved. And my great-granddaddy's beer brought him right to it. The bastard couldn't stand seeing that can in his perfect Disneyland brewery. Stooped right down to..." He stopped, eyes wide. "I don't know what you're talking about."

"Yes, you do," I said, taking a step back. "That's why you went there. And Billy refused to give you the recipes and was rude. He was going to go back and tell Simon what you'd done. You couldn't stand the humiliation, so you killed him."

"Got the recipes, too," Max said, his eyes cold. He reached behind him and fumbled for a moment, then he pulled a gun out of what seemed like thin air.

"Crap," Quinn murmured beside me. I could see her hand stray to the pepper spray in her pocket, then move away as she reconsidered. She looked at me. "Plan B?"

"How did you do it?" I asked Max, playing for time.

"I shoved him in one of the tanks here and sprayed him with chemicals," he said. "Then I took him over to Sweetwater and stuck him in a barrel."

"Nice," I said. "So suspicion falls on Simon."

"Serves him right," he said. "And now, ladies... if you'll just come over here."

"I wouldn't do that if I were you," Quinn said. "Folks

know we're here. Suspicion will come right back and land on you if anything happens to us."

I realized Quinn was lying. I'd been so busy thinking about what I wanted to say that I hadn't remembered to call Tobias; I think having Quinn with me gave me a false sense of security. And I never expected him to confess, anyway. Had she called Peter? I hadn't heard her do it, but maybe she had before we left?

"I can deal with that," he said. "Just have to get rid of your vehicle. Not a problem. Who drove?"

"I did," I admitted.

"Give me the keys," he ordered, suddenly seeming a lot less tipsy.

I fumbled in my pocket and pulled out my key chain. I hesitated, and he cocked the gun. "Okay," I said, and took a step forward and handed them over.

"Phones, too," he said, crushing my hope of a last-minute call to Tobias. Or 911, which would be a better call.

Quinn and I both handed over our cell phones. He glanced at them and shoved them in his back pocket.

"Good. Now, go that way," he said, waving us toward a door in the corner of the brewery. "Hands up," he said sharply as Quinn's hand moved toward her pocket again.

We raised our hands and walked to the door. He stepped in front of us, gun still trained on me, then pulled the door open. Inside were pallets of cans waiting for shipment; there were no windows or other doors.

"Get in," he said. We did as he asked; then, without another word, he slammed the door behind us. I heard the lock snick, and then footsteps moving away.

"Nicely done," Quinn said as we stood in the darkness. "No phone, no light, and a drunk murderer with a gun hiding your truck so that he can kill us without getting caught."

"Did you call Peter?" I asked.

"I meant to, but we got talking... I'm such an idiot."

"So am I," I said.

"You didn't call Tobias?"

"I was going to wait until the last minute so he couldn't tell me not to, and then... well, I forgot."

"So we're hosed," she said.

"Let's not get too pessimistic," I cautioned her.

"Really, Lucy?" she asked. "What's Plan B, then? Or Plan C?"

"I don't know yet," I admitted. "Let me think."

I'd gotten a glimpse of the room's interior before he closed the door. It was filled with cans... pallets of them. Was there some way to use that to our advantage? As I sat there, my eyes adjusted to the gloom. Light poured around the edges of the door, helping illuminate the space enough to make out the dark hulk of the pallet stacks. I felt around for a light switch, but there wasn't one. There didn't appear to be a light fixture in the middle of the room, either; I swept my hand through the air, but encountered no string or chain. Which wasn't really surprising, as Max was clearly running a bare-bones operation.

I focused on the door. "How's your kicking?" I asked.

"Why?"

"I thought you might be able to take down that door," I said.

"It opens inward," she pointed out. "That makes it rather harder."

"Give it a whirl?" I suggested.

A moment later, I sensed movement and a loud "thud." The door quivered, but stayed firm. She tried a second and third time, but there was nothing. "It's a solid door," she said. "And a deadbolt. How about Plan D?"

"I do have a Plan D," I realized suddenly. "We just have to restack some pallets of cans. Are you in?"

She swore under her breath a little. "I don't have a Plan E, so I guess I don't have a choice."

"We have to hurry," I said. "I don't think we'll have a second chance once he gets back." I told her my plan.

"It might work," she said grudgingly. "But we'd better get cracking."

We raced against time, sweating and praying Pfeiffer would take his time as we lugged cans off of the pallets and then restacked them all next to the doorway. It seemed to take forever.

"Are they high enough yet?" Quinn panted when we got the levered the last pallet above the height of the doorframe.

"Lord, I hope so," I said. "And I hope like heck this plan works, or we're toast. The only thing we're missing is a decoy."

"How do we do that?"

"With clothes," I said. I pulled off my T-shirt and jeans and felt my way to the pallets at the end of the room. I tucked the jeans into the stack at about waist height, so that they stretched down to the floor, and then arranged my T-shirt above it. "Good thing it's not cold," I said, as I walked back to the door in my underwear. "Ready?"

"I'm ready," she said. We made our final preparations and took our places, hearts in our throats, hoping my crazy plan would work.

21

I have no idea how long it was before we heard footsteps in the brewery again. It felt like both forever and not nearly enough time, and we jumped at every creak and whirr from the brewery. Despite the dearth of clothing, I was sweating with nerves, hoping that my plan was going to work. We weren't sure if we could hear Pfeiffer coming, so we'd positioned ourselves while we waited. My feet hurt from standing on concrete, and I knew Quinn must feel the same.

Finally, just when I was about to scream, I heard the deadbolt snick back. I could smell my own fear as the doorknob turned, and the door swung inward, the light making me wince.

I saw the gun first, trained on the back of the room. And then everything happened at once.

I pushed the button on the pepper spray, aiming it through the hole in the pallets I'd arranged to hide behind so that it hit Max right in the face. His hands instinctively went to his eyes. At the same time, Quinn pushed over the pallets we'd stacked up next to the door. I heard a grunt and the rattle of cans hitting the floor. I raced around the stacked pallets to where Max writhed on the hard floor.

He still had the gun in his hand. The door was only half-open, held open by his legs. Quinn rounded at the same time; seeing the gun in his hand, she launched herself at him, pushing his arm down. As I watched, his wrist twisted, moving the gun bit by bit toward Quinn's head.

"No!" I yelled, and he fired. The bullet ricocheted around the room, puncturing cans. Beer hissed out of holes in cans. I heard the gun cocking again, and leaped forward, coming down with my right foot on top of his hand—and the gun.

Another bullet shot out of the barrel, puncturing another line of cans, and the smell of beer intensified.

Max swore. I looked down; his hand was pinned to the ground, the gun in it smashed between the concrete and my boot.

"Let me go," Quinn growled.

"No way," he grunted back.

"Now," she barked. As she did, I made out her hand rising, then coming down hard on Max's neck.

His body went limp.

I kicked the gun away from his flaccid hand and scrambled after it.

"Are you okay?" I asked as my hand closed around the gun's grip.

"Plan D isn't my favorite, and I never ever want to do that again, but at least it worked," she said. "You okay with the gun? I'm going to go find a rope."

"I'll be here," I said.

~

BY THE TIME ROOSTER ARRIVED, Pfeiffer had come to, still

struggling to breathe. Quinn had tied him up, and I'd put my clothes back on. She'd found a phone in the brewery and called 911 as soon as we'd gotten Pfeiffer incapacitated.

"What in the name of..." Rooster started as he pulled open the door to the storage room and took in the scene.

"We'll tell you all about it," I said. "But first you might want to call the station and tell Opal to let Simon go."

"What? Why?"

"Max here confessed to murdering Felix and Billy," Quinn said. "And if we can find my phone—and Lucy's truck—you'll have it all on record."

"You're welcome," I added. "And do you have handcuffs on you? I'm getting tired of holding this gun."

He blinked at us for a few minutes. "What are y'all doin' here in the first place?"

"Like I said, it's a long story. He locked us in here; we managed to get his gun away before he killed us, but I'd be happy to be out of this storage room sooner than later, if that's okay with you," Quinn informed him.

"You're sure he confessed?"

Quinn and I shared a look.

"Like I said, we'll be happy to tell you all about it. But first I want to get out of here and find my truck."

"IF I DIDN'T LOVE you, I'd kill you," Tobias said when he got to the farm two hours later. We'd gotten a ride back to the town with one of the deputies and found my truck using a locator app on Quinn's computer; Pfeiffer had driven it down into a ravine not far from the farm. They still hadn't towed it out yet, and it was still evidence, so I was truck-less for the foreseeable future, but at least they had a recording of our conversation with Max Pfeiffer.

Now, Tobias pulled me into a fierce hug, and then he told me off. "What were you thinking?"

"I wasn't," I said. "You're right. Quinn told me the same thing. We were going to call, and then we both got distracted..."

"She's no better," Tobias said. "She didn't call anyone either. You were almost killed!"

"You're right," I said, touched that he cared so much. "I'm sorry."

"Tell me what happened," he said, and as we sat down on the front porch with Chuck and the two kittens in our laps, I relayed everything that had happened.

"So Billy was killed because he didn't take the job," Tobias said.

"Pretty much," I said. "Although Billy wasn't a very nice person. Not that that excuses what Max did, but still..."

He sighed. "It's tragic. But at least Simon won't be in jail for a crime he didn't commit."

"True," I said.

As we sat, contemplating what had happened, Ed's truck came down the driveway. "Oh, good," I said. "Maybe he can help us with the camera."

Tobias and I each scooped up a kitten and walked out to greet Ed as he stepped out of his truck. "I was hoping to see you today!" I said. "I had another run-in with the Ulrich House last night."

"I can see that," he said, and spotted the kittens in our arms. "Whatcha got there?"

"Some stray kittens we found," I said. "The mama cat's that gray tabby; we're hoping to catch her, too, so we can take care of her."

"You're good folks," Ed said approvingly.

"I looked for the camera, but I couldn't find it."

"That's because I hid it behind some ball moss, just in case someone went lookin'," he said. "I heard you had some excitement today, by the way."

"That's one word for it," I told him. "But all's well that ends well. Except for Felix and Billy, that is."

"Sad state of affairs," he said. "But at least we know we don't have a murderer runnin' around town anymore. Although we might still have a vandal on the loose," he said, reaching up into the branches of a crape myrtle and pushing a few bits of ball moss aside to retrieve a camera.

"What's on it?" I asked.

"We'll see," he said, hitting a few buttons so that it played on fast forward. I could see myself walking by the house, and later, when it was darker, a raccoon on the porch, and after that, what looked like mama cat. A deer wandered by, too, nosing at the grass on the side of the house. And then a person turned up, swinging a sledgehammer at the posts of the porch.

"Whoa," Tobias said. "We got someone."

"But can you see a face?"

"Let me slow it down," Ed said. Tobias and I peered over his shoulder as he slowed it down. The face was in shadow, a flashlight beam focused on the sledgehammer. Then he shifted hands, and the flashlight illuminated a face for a split second.

"Is that who I think it is?" I asked.

"It sure is," Ed said. "And we are goin' to have some words."

Tobias and I exchanged glances.

The person who had been sabotaging the renovation project was Nick.

"BUT WHY WOULD HE DO THAT?" I asked when we got back to the house. Ed had left to talk to Nick, and we were now sitting on the couch in my living room with two bottles of Bluff lager, theorizing. I knew the Oktoberfest market started soon, but Tobias had offered to help me... and besides, I needed a few minutes to breathe.

"I have no idea. If he vandalized the scaffolding, that didn't end up well for him; he broke his leg."

"And the Ulrich house almost fell down on his head," I said. "Do you think he was trying to make the job seem so dangerous that his dad agreed to send him back to school?"

"It's not the brightest idea in the world, but he is a teenager..."

I sighed. "Too much excitement for one week, if you ask me. Any word back on the feed sample, by the way?"

"I haven't checked my messages!" He pulled his phone from his back pocket and checked voicemail. His face looked grave when he hung up. "It's ergot, all right. We need to talk to Adriana and find out who she sold her barley to."

"I'm guessing it's whoever's supplying feed to Lotte Heinrich," I said.

"I'll call her right now and tell her to stop selling it."

"I bought some the other day and gave everyone a little," I said. "Will they be okay?"

"They should be," Tobias said, "but don't give them any more."

"Of course not." I stood up and stretched. "While you're doing that, I'm going to start loading the truck—your truck, if you don't mind." I was glad I'd unloaded the back of mine before driving it to visit Max Pfeiffer.

"I'll come help you in a minute," he said. "You sure you want to do this tonight?'

"Those soaps aren't going to sell themselves," I said. "Besides, I want to check in with Simon. And Teena."

"I wish that girl would go to college this fall. She deferred because of Felix, her dad told me the other day."

"Maybe she can undefer, if that's a word, and go this fall after all, even if it is a little late. I'll suggest she'll look into it, for what that's worth."

"Good luck with that," Tobias said.

"I know. You take care of the kittens, all right?"

"Of course," he said. "They have names yet?"

"Lucky and Smoky," I said.

"You're keeping them?"

I looked down at the kittens and smiled. The gray one was behind Chuck, batting lazily at his tail, and the orange tabby lay curled up on his back in between Chuck's front paws. "I'm not sure I have a choice."

A COLD FRONT swept through Buttercup just in time for Oktoberfest to open that evening. Tobias helped me set up, then headed off to retrieve dinner for both of us as I faced the onslaught of townspeople who had heard a little bit about what had happened earlier that afternoon. I glanced across the square to where Quinn's Blue Onion booth was; it was equally crowded with curious people. The Sweetwater booth was open, too, but I hadn't spotted Simon or Teena yet.

"So Max Pfeiffer killed both of them?" asked Serafine Alexandre, who had left her mead booth to check in with me—and bring me a cup of mead. "I figured after today, you needed it," she explained as she handed it to me. I took a grateful sip of the cool, sweet drink and smiled at my friend. Her long black braids were swept up into a kind of crown above her high-cheekboned face, and with her long purple skirt and silk spaghetti-strap top, she looked exotic as always, particularly for downtown Buttercup.

"He did," I said.

"And Sweetwater's going to survive?" she asked.

"I hope so," I said. "I'll do what I can to support them."

"Me too," she agreed. "They've put so much into it, and are really making something special. I feel bad about Felix, though."

"So do I. And the assistant brewer."

"It's awful," Serafine said. "I'm so glad they caught the killer. How are the bees, by the way?"

"They seem to be humming along," I said.

"I'll come check them for you this week, if you like."

"I'd love that," I said.

"I'll bring some more beeswax, too." She glanced at my dwindling candle supply. "It looks like you might need it."

I gave her a hug and thanked her, then turned to the next person in line, who was Fannie, the owner of the antique shop on the square. Following her came a number of other Buttercuppians, most of whom purchased something before heading out to spread the news of what had happened.

The oompah band was playing a sprightly tune, the chilled breeze was swinging the fairy lights, and the smell of roasting bratwurst and kettle corn was making me salivate by the time the stream of curiosity-seekers died down. Tobias had been waylaid, too; it took him the better part of three-quarters of an hour to make it back to the stall, by which time almost all of my soaps were sold.

I'd just finished the bratwurst he'd brought me when Simon and Teena walked over to greet me.

"Hey, guys!" I said. "Good to see you out and about," I told Simon, who was looking better than I'd seen him the last few days.

"I hear I have you to thank for finding my brother's killer," Simon said.

"And Teena here," I told him. "If she hadn't given me a few clues, I'm not sure I would have put things together."

"I'm glad you did. I can't bring my brother back, but at least I know justice has been served."

"I'm sorry you lost your recipes."

"We didn't, actually," Simon said. "I have a copy in the safe."

"Whew." I was relieved. "Are you going to be able to do it solo?"

"I'm short my brother, of course, and my assistant brewer, but if Teena doesn't go back to school this fall, I'm hoping she'll stick around and take on more responsibility... And since we just signed a contract to join Brewlific, we'll have breweries across the country sharing their recipes and making ours."

"You signed?"

"Felix wouldn't have wanted it, I know, but it was the right thing to keep the business going," Simon said. "I think we'll have a bright future now."

"I'm so glad," I said. "I know how hard you've worked."

"And if you're interested in experimenting with growing hops, or maybe selling some of your dewberries for a spring brew..."

"Or maybe some honey once you get the bees up and running," Teena suggested.

"I'd love that," I said. "Thank you for thinking of me."

"In fact," he said, "as a thank you for figuring things out, I'd like to offer you a stake in the company." He gave me a sad smile. "Since without you, there'd be no company."

"You don't have to do that!" I said.

"I know," he said, "but I want to."

Did I feel comfortable having a stake in Sweetwater? I wasn't sure yet; I hadn't done what I'd done for money, but to help out and put things right. "Can I think about it?"

"Of course," he said. "The offer stands. Let me know anytime."

"Thank you," I said. "And I'm so sorry about your brother... but I'm glad you're moving on. Oh, by the way... I think I know who fouled that barrel of beer."

"Really?" Simon perked up. "Who?"

"Nick Schmidt bought sulfur down at Heinrich Feed not too long ago, and he was in the brewery that day. I can't say for sure, but I'd say that's your best bet."

"But why?" he asked.

I looked at Teena. "I think he was jealous of your brother."

"Oh," Simon said, looking at Teena. "I see. I hear he may be in other trouble, too, so I suppose that's not surprising."

"What did you hear?"

"Apparently he took pay-offs from the construction company out of Houston to sabotage Ed Mandel's projects so that they would get the Buttercup Bank job."

"What?"

"Too bad he broke his leg in the process. Or maybe not," Simon said. "I think he thought it would be a double benefit; his dad would be convinced that the construction business was too dangerous for his son, and he'd get a kickback besides."

"That's horrible!" I said.

"Well, the bank just gave the job to Ed, so there's some good news," Simon said. "And I know he'll be hiring new help soon, so if you know anyone who's good in construction..."

"I'll keep an ear out," I said. "I'm glad he got the job, but I hope that doesn't mean my project will be delayed..."

Ed walked up to the stall. "I'll get it done," he said. He held out his hand to Simon. "Congratulations. I just heard the news about your new business venture."

"Thanks," Simon said, shaking the offered hand. "And congratulations on your new contract."

"Thank you," Ed said, then turned to me. "I heard about what you and Quinn did, and your place just turned into my top priority. I told the folks at the bank that I couldn't do a thing until I knew your little house was in tip-top shape."

"Really?" I asked. "Thanks so much!"

"It's the least I could do," he said. "After all, I brought a vandal onto your property."

"Poor boy," I said. "Will he go to jail?"

"I don't know, but he needs some help," Ed said. "And I won't be hiring him again."

"I'll bet not," I said. I was glad he was just a saboteur and not a murderer, though.

"I think you should go walk around for a while," Teena said, then turned to Simon. "Mind if I take over for Lucy for the night?"

"I would be delighted," he said. "It's the least we can do." He turned to Teena. "And if I can get things going with Brewlific, I'd like to help pay for your college, as long as you'll come intern for us in the summer and take a job with us your first year out."

"What?" Teena turned pink. "Really?"

"Really. Go learn all about the world of marketing, and then help me make Sweetwater a household name."

"I'd love that!" she said. "Thank you!" She went to hug him then held back, blushing harder. I resisted the urge to roll my eyes; did Teena already have another crush on an older man?

"Are you sure you want to take over the booth?" I asked, hoping to end the awkward moment.

"Absolutely," she said. "Just show me what to do!"

As Simon headed back to Sweetwater's booth, where I saw Beth Collins waiting for him (she gave me a quick wave), I got Teena up to speed. By the time Tobias came back with food, I was ready to go.

"What do I do with all of this?" he asked, looking at the bag of goodies he'd brought back.

"Give it to Teena," I said. "Except for the beer. That's mine," I said. "First stop is the Blue Onion stall; I need more lebkuchen. And maybe a Bienenstich."

"You got it," he said, and kissed me on the forehead. And arm in arm, we walked through the Buttercup Oktoberfest, enjoying the cool fall breeze from the north, greeting our friends and neighbors, and eating bratwurst, pretzels, and lebkuchen until we could barely move, while the band played and the lights sparkled overhead.

It was a magical evening, and, I hoped, just one of many, many more to come.

MORE BOOKS BY KAREN MACINERNEY

To download a free book and receive members-only outtakes, short stories, recipes, and updates, join Karen's Reader's Circle at www.karenmacinerney.com! You can also join her on Facebook.

And don't forget to follow her on BookBub to get newsflashes on new releases!

The Dewberry Farm Mysteries

The Gray Whale Inn Mysteries

Brush With Death
Death Runs Adrift
Whale of a Crime
Claws for Alarm
Scone Cold Dead
Cookbook: The Gray Whale Inn Kitchen
Blueberry Blues (A Gray Whale Inn Short Story)
Pumpkin Pied (A Gray Whale Inn Short Story)
Iced Inn (A Gray Whale Inn Short Story)

The Margie Peterson Mysteries
Mother's Day Out
Mother Knows Best
Mother's Little Helper

Tales of an Urban Werewolf
Howling at the Moon
On the Prowl
Leader of the Pack

Six Merry Little Murders: A Cozy Christmas Bundle
(October 2019)

And coming Fall/Winter 2019... a new paranormal cozy series!
More details coming soon...

RECIPES

BIENENSTICH (BEE STING CAKE)

I first had this cake in Munich, and I've loved it ever since. So does Lucy, oddly enough. :)

Ingredients:

Cake

1 3/4 cup flour
2 Tbsp sugar
2 1/4 tsp yeast (1 packet)
pinch of salt
1 egg (at room temperature)
1/4 cup melted butter
1/3 cup milk (at room temperature)

Topping

1/4 cup butter
1 Tbsp honey
6 Tbsp sugar

1 1/2 Tbsp heavy whipping cream
3/4 cup sliced almonds

Filling

2 cups heavy whipping cream
1 3.4-oz. packet vanilla pudding mix

Instructions:

Preheat the oven to 350. Combine the flour, sugar, yeast, salt, butter, egg, and milk in a large bowl, kneading the dough a few times until it becomes smooth.

Remove the dough from the bowl and spray the bowl with cooking spray, then return the dough to the bowl. Cover with a towel and let it rise for 30 minutes.

While the cake dough is rising, make the topping by melting the butter, honey, and sugar in a small saucepan over medium heat. When the butter has melted, add the cream and stir until the sugar is dissolved. Remove the saucepan from heat and stir in sliced almonds.

Spray or grease an 8×8 baking dish and then place a sheet of parchment paper in the dish so that the edges hang over the sides. Roll out the dough and press it into the dish, then prick the dough several times with a fork. Pour the almond topping onto dough, spreading it out evenly. Bake the cake for 35 minutes; the topping will be golden brown when the cake is done.

Let the cake cool for a few minutes and use the parchment

paper to remove it from the baking dish. When you can touch the topping with your fingers, use a long serrated knife to cut the cake in two layers.

Place the top layer on a sheet of parchment paper and use the same knife to cut the top layer into nine equal-sized pieces. (It's much easier to cut the top layer when it's still a bit warm.)

Add the pudding powder to the heavy cream and whip to stiff peaks, then spread the filling over the bottom cake layer. Gently place the top layer onto the cream filling piece by piece. Chill the cake for 1 hour or until the filling is set.

When you're ready to serve the cake, slice the Bienenstich gently with a sharp knife while you hold the top lightly, being careful not to not to use too much pressure (or else the filling will spill out). Guten Appetit!

LEBKUCHEN (GINGERBREAD) OKTOBERFEST HEARTS

Ingredients:

3/4 cup softened (not warm) butter
1/4 cup brown sugar
1 tablespoon ground ginger
1 teaspoon ground cinnamon
1/4 teaspoon ground nutmeg
1/4 teaspoon ground cloves
1 teaspoon finely grated lemon zest
1/2 teaspoon finely grated orange zest
3/4 cup molasses
1/3 cup honey
2 medium eggs, beaten
3 to 4 cups all-purpose flour
1 teaspoon baking soda
1/4 teaspoon salt

Egg white for brushing

Royal Icing for decorating

Instructions:

Cream butter and sugar in a large bowl until light and fluffy, then add spices and zests, beating until they are incorporated. In a small saucepan over medium-high heat, heat molasses and honey until boiling and allow to cool for 10 minutes. Add the molasses mixture to the creamed butter, stirring constantly, then beat in the eggs one by one and combine thoroughly.

Sift 3 cups flour, baking soda and salt together in a large bowl and stir into the butter/molasses mixture one cup at a time, adding as much of the remaining flour as needed to get a soft but not sticky dough. Shape dough into a ball, cover with plastic wrap, and chill overnight.

Preheat oven to 350 degrees. Roll out chilled dough to about 1/3-inch thick. Using cutters or working freehand, cut the dough into whatever shapes you have in mind (hearts are typical for Oktoberfest; if you're adding ribbon to the top, as is traditional in Germany, don't forget to add a hole for the ribbon). Brush cookies with lightly beaten egg white, place on a parchment-covered baking sheet with plenty of space between the cookies, and bake for 12 to 15 minutes. Try not to let the edges brown!

To decorate Oktoberfest Hearts, wait until completely cooled and decorate with a piped stiff royal icing, made from a mixture of slightly beaten egg whites, a little lemon juice and confectioner's (powdered or icing) sugar added gradually until the icing becomes stiff and stands in peaks. You can color some of the icing if you like (blue is traditional), or leave it white. In Germany, words like "I love you" or "Oktoberfest" are frequently piped, along with a decorative border. Have fun!

CHOCOLATE GLAZED LEBKUCHEN

Ingredients:

Lebkuchen

1/2 + 1/3 cup dark brown sugar, packed
2/3 cup honey
Scant 1/4 cup butter, softened
Finely grated zest of 1 orange
2 1/2 cups flour
1 1/4 cups ground almonds
1 tbsp cocoa powder
2 1/2 tsp ground ginger
1 1/2 tsp ground cinnamon
1/2 tsp ground allspice
1/4 tsp ground cloves
1/4 tsp ground nutmeg
1/2 tsp salt
1/2 tsp baking powder
1/4 tsp baking soda
2 medium eggs

Glaze

1 1/2 cups powdered sugar, sifted
2 tbsp water
7oz. dark chocolate, chopped

Instructions:

Combine the sugar, honey, butter and orange zest in a large bowl and beat with an electric mixer until smooth. In a separate bowl, sift together the flour, ground almonds, cocoa powder, spices, salt, baking powder and baking soda and set aside.

Add the eggs to the sugar mixture one at a time, beating well after each addition, then add the flour mixture to the sugar mixture a cup at a time, mixing until well combined.

When the dough is mixed, cover the bowl and place in the fridge for half an hour (preferably overnight).

Preheat the oven to 350 degrees and line two baking sheets with parchment paper. Scoop out balls of dough using a measuring spoon or coffee scoop, about 1 1/2 tbsp at a time, and roll dough balls between slightly damp hands until round and smooth. Place on the baking sheets with ample space between them, flattening them slightly with your fingers.

Bake cookies for about 15 minutes; when they are done, they will be firm and lightly browned, and a toothpick inserted into the center will out clean. Transfer the cookies to a wire rack and allow to cool completely.

When the cookies are cooled, measure the powdered sugar into a small bowl and gradually mix in enough of the water to form a slightly runny icing (if it is too wet it will run off the cookies). Place a wire rack on a baking sheet.

Dip the tops of the cookies into the glaze, allow the excess to drip off, and then place them right-side up on the wire rack to set.

Once the sugar glaze has set, melt the chocolate, either in a double boiler or in short bursts in the microwave (check it often), then pour it into a small bowl. Line a baking sheet with parchment paper. Dip the bottoms of the cookies into the chocolate, allowing the excess to drip off, then place the cookies chocolate-side-down on the parchment paper to set. Once the glaze is set, store the cookies in an airtight container.

GOAT MILK FLAN

Ingredients:

Nonstick cooking spray
1/3 cup granulated sugar
2 cups goat's milk (you can use cow's milk instead, if you're
not a fan of goat's milk)
1/2 cup plus 1 tablespoon superfine sugar
3 egg yolks, beaten
2 whole eggs, beaten
1/4 teaspoon vanilla extract

Instructions:

Preheat oven to 350 degrees and lightly grease four 6-ounce
ramekins with nonstick cooking spray.

Add the granulated sugar to a small saucepan set over high
heat and let the sugar melt without stirring. As it melts,
gently swirl the pan around to make sure it melts evenly.
When the sugar has turned to caramel and is dark amber in

color, carefully divide the caramel evenly among the ramekins. (If your caramel isn't working and you want an easier approach, you can simply pour a tablespoon or two of dark corn syrup into the bottom of each ramekin).

Add the milk and the superfine sugar to a saucepan and bring the mixture to a gentle simmer. As the milk heats, add the egg yolks, whole eggs and vanilla to a large mixing bowl, whisking together until foamy. Add a little of the hot milk to temper the eggs, stirring to combine, then gradually add the rest of the milk so it doesn't cook the eggs. Once the milk is completely incorporated, stir the mixture well and then divide it evenly among the four ramekins.

Line a deep baking dish or roasting pan with a kitchen towel and carefully place the ramekins on top. Place the dish in the oven, then fill it with hot water so it comes 3/4 of the way up the sides of the ramekins.

Bake until the custards are set, about 35 minutes, and remove the ramekins from the oven and allow to cool. (I often use tongs or potholders to take them out of the roasting pan and cool them on a wire rack; they can be slippery, though, so be careful.) Chill flans in the fridge before inverting onto a plate to serve.

GERMAN PRETZELS

Ingredients:

Pretzels

4 cups all-purpose flour
2 teaspoons salt
1 teaspoon sugar
1 cup lukewarm water
4 1/2 teaspoons (2 pkgs) active dry yeast
3 tbsp butter
Coarse salt for sprinkling

Baking Soda Bath

1/2 cup baking soda
2 quarts water

Instructions:

In a small bowl, dissolve the yeast in the lukewarm water. In a large mixing bowl, combine flour and salt. Form a well in the middle of the flour mixture. Add the sugar to the center of the well, then pour the yeast mixture into the well. Let rest for 15 minutes before mixing.

After 15 minutes, add the softened butter to the mixing bowl and knead everything to a smooth dough by hand or with the dough hook on a standing mixer, adding a bit more water (not too much) if dough is too dry. Form dough into a ball and let dough rest for 30 minutes.

Line a cookie sheet with parchment paper. Cut the ball of dough into twelve equal parts, then with your hands, roll each piece on an unfloured, clean table or countertop to a dough rope of about 20 inches (not less), tapering the dough at the ends. Try not to overwork the dough; if it gets too warm as you roll it out, it might tear.

To form a pretzel shape, place a dough rope on the parchment-lined cookie sheet so that it creates a letter "U". Take both ends of the "U" and cross them over each other twice to form a twist, then bring the twist down and place it over the bottom curve of the "U".

Place the pretzels in the refrigerator (I like to put them on parchment-paper-lined pans that I later use for baking), uncovered, for about an hour.

Preheat the oven to 400 F. Fill a large pot with water until 3/4 full and bring the water to a boil. Carefully and slowly add the baking soda to the boiling water; stand back a bit, as the baking soda will bubble up violently for a moment when it hits the water.

Using a slotted spoon, gently drop each pretzel into the bath for ten seconds, then turn the pretzel over for another ten seconds. Place the finished pretzels on a baking sheet lined with parchment paper.

Score each pretzel once with a razor blade or sharp knife and sprinkle with coarse salt. Bake the pretzels for about 15 to 20 minutes, depending on how dark you like them.

FARM-FRESH MOZZARELLA CHEESE

Ingredients:

1 gallon milk, NOT ultra-pasteurized
1 1/2 tsp citric acid
1/4 rennet tablet or 1/4 tsp single strength liquid rennet
1 tsp cheese salt (adjust to taste). Kosher and sea salt
work, too!

Instructions:

Clear your work area of all food, wipe it down, and use
antibacterial cleaner before starting.

Crush 1/4 tablet of rennet and dissolve in 1/4 cup of cool non-
chlorinated water, or add 1/4 tsp single strength liquid
rennet to the water. Set aside to use later. Add 1 1/2 tsp. of
citric acid to 1 cup cool water and pour into a large pot, then
quickly add cold milk and mix it in well.

Heat the milk slowly until it reaches 90°F. (As the temperature approaches 90°F, you may notice the milk beginning to curdle slightly). If the milk doesn't seem to be separating and forming a curd, you may need to increase this temp to 95°F or even 100F.

At 90°F (or when curds are properly formed—I'd recommend googling a picture), remove the pot from the burner and slowly add the prepared rennet to the milk. Stir from top to bottom for approximately 30 seconds, then stop. Cover the pot and leave it undisturbed for 5 minutes.

After 5 minutes, check the curd. It should look like custard, with a clear separation between the curds and whey. If the curd is too soft or the whey looks milky, let it sit for longer, up to 30 additional minutes.

Using a long knife, cut the curds into a 1" checkerboard pattern, then place the pot back on the stove and heat the curds to 105°F while slowly stirring them with your ladle. Take the pot off the burner and continue stirring slowly for 2-5 minutes; the longer you stir, the firmer the cheese. With a slotted spoon, scoop curds into a colander and press the curd gently with your hand, pouring off as much whey as possible. (Rubber gloves help with the heat.)

From the colander, transfer the curds to a heat- and microwave-safe bowl, mix one teaspoon of salt into the curds, and microwave the curd for 1 minute. Drain off additional whey, then work the cheese with a spoon or your hands until it is cool enough to touch (again, rubber gloves will help). Microwave the curds twice more for 35 seconds each, repeating the kneading and draining each time.

Knead the curd as you would bread dough; after a few minutes, remove the curd from the bowl and continue kneading until the curd smooth and shiny. (If it cools before it reaches this point, put it in the microwave in increments of 15 seconds to heat it back up.) When the cheese is soft and pliable enough to stretch, if you feel it needs it, add a bit more salt, then stretch the cheese like taffy (you'll want to do this many times) to create the fibers that make it mozzarella.

Knead the cheese back into a big ball until it is smooth and shiny. To cool it quickly, place it in a bowl of ice water and refrigerate. When cheese is cold, it will last for several days wrapped in plastic, but is best when eaten fresh. (Preferably with homegrown tomatoes and basil. Mmm.)

ACKNOWLEDGMENTS

First, many thanks to my family, not just for putting up with me, but for continuing to come up with creative ways to kill people. (You should see the looks we get in restaurants.)

Special thanks to (512) Brewing Company and Adelbert's Brewery in Austin, who were so helpful when I asked, "If you were going to do someone in here, how would you do it?" I learned a ton about the way the craft brewing business works from (512)'s Head Brewer Owen Sawyer... he also gave me some great explanations of the brewing process and some amazing beer. Mmm. Thank you also to Andy Krell for all of his hard work accompanying me on those grueling tours, not to mention the extensive beer sampling.

Thank you also to the folks at Trianon Coffee for keeping me caffeinated and providing wonderful company and feedback... especially, you, Chloe Payne, and your darling Violet! Thank you also to Gene Smithson and Jason Brenizer for being my writing buddies/morale boosters here in Austin, and to CeeCee James for just being awesome. (Read CeeCee's series if you haven't!)

Thanks always to the MacInerney Mystery Mavens, who are indispensable with all manner of things, from covers to concepts to early reads... what would I do without you? Thank you also to Kim Killion for her amazing cover art and to Angelika Offenwanger for keeping me from embarrassing myself. Vielen Dank! :)

And finally, thank you to YOU, and to ALL of the wonderful readers who make Dewberry Farm possible, especially my fabulous Facebook community. You keep me going!

ABOUT THE AUTHOR

Karen is the housework-impaired, award-winning author of multiple mystery series, and her victims number well into the double digits. She lives in Austin, Texas with her sassy family, Tristan, and Little Bit (a.k.a. Dog #1 and Dog #2).

Feel free to visit Karen's web site at www. karenmacinerney.com, where you can download a free book and sign up for her Readers' Circle to receive subscriber-only short stories, deleted scenes, recipes and other bonus material. You can also find her on Facebook (she spends an inordinate amount of time there), where Karen loves getting to know her readers, answering questions, and offering quirky, behind-the-scenes looks at the writing process (and life in general).

P. S. Don't forget to follow Karen on BookBub to get news-flashes on new releases!

www.karenmacinerney.com
karen@karenmacinerney.com

facebook.com/AuthorKarenMacInerney

twitter.com/KarenMacInerney

Made in the USA
San Bernardino,
CA